More than anything, he needed to win her trust.

"You do realize that by asking about this killer, he might come after you?"

She winced, her only reaction. "I do. But if I help catch him, it'll be worth it."

"Why is it worth risking your life?" he asked.

She looked away this time and absentmindedly rubbed her finger over the scar on her wrist. A telltale sign he was right. And one that made him more curious about how she'd gotten that scar.

Concerned about her now, he lowered his voice. "Ginny, tell me what you know." He reached for her arm to trace the burn scar with his finger, but she jerked it away and crossed the room to the window. For a moment, she stood staring outside at the rain drizzling against the windowpane.

She looked pale, sad and frightened. But beautiful, like a lost child in a storm. The instinct to pull her into his arms pulsed through Griff, so strongly that he fisted his hands by his sides.

Pushing her would only make her run away.

PROTECTIVE ORDER

USA TODAY Bestselling Author
RITA HERRON

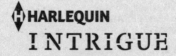

HARLEQUIN
INTRIGUE

To all those counselors who work as victims' advocates for
abused women. God bless you.

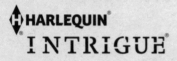

INTRIGUE

ISBN-13: 978-1-335-13671-8

Protective Order

Recycling programs
for this product may
not exist in your area.

USA TODAY bestselling author **Rita Herron** wrote her first book when she was twelve but didn't think real people grew up to be writers. Now she writes so she doesn't have to get a real job. A former kindergarten teacher and workshop leader, she traded storytelling to kids for writing romance, and now she writes romantic comedies and romantic suspense. Rita lives in Georgia with her family. She loves to hear from readers, so please visit her website, ritaherron.com.

Books by Rita Herron

Harlequin Intrigue

A Badge of Honor Mystery

Mysterious Abduction
Left to Die
Protective Order

Badge of Justice

Redemption at Hawk's Landing
Safe at Hawk's Landing
Hideaway at Hawk's Landing
Hostage at Hawk's Landing

The Heroes of Horseshoe Creek

Lock, Stock and McCullen
McCullen's Secret Son
Roping Ray McCullen
Warrior Son
The Missing McCullen
The Last McCullen

Cold Case at Camden Crossing
Cold Case at Carlton's Canyon
Cold Case at Cobra Creek
Cold Case in Cherokee Crossing

Visit the Author Profile page at Harlequin.com.

CAST OF CHARACTERS

Reese Taggart, aka Ginny Bagwell—All she wants is revenge against her stalker ex-boyfriend for killing her sister. Until she meets sexy firefighter Griff Maverick.

Griff Maverick—As firefighter and arson investigator, he's determined to find out Ginny Bagwell's secrets.

Joy Norris—She was strangled, her body left in her fiery apartment. Did Reese's stalker kill Joy, or did she fall victim to another predator?

Robert Bouldercrest—Reese's ex swore she'd never escape him. And he will kill anyone who keeps him from getting her back.

Thad Ridgen—Joy was the only holdout to making this real estate developer a millionaire. Did he kill her for money?

William Roberts—Is he really Robert Bouldercrest?

Prologue

He'd kill her if he found her.

But Reese Taggart couldn't go back. Not to being smothered and held captive by his anger and his erratic mood swings. Not to pleasing him when that was impossible.

Not to a life without friends and a house where she had to follow his rules or be punished.

She tugged the ball cap over her head and struggled to stay in the shadows as she climbed in her car and pulled away from the gas station. A big burly man wearing a hoodie was watching her from the gas pump.

Tension gathered in her belly. Had Robert paid the man to find her?

Shivering, she pressed the accelerator and sped onto the highway. Nerves on edge, she looked over her shoulder to see if the man had followed.

Finally, when she veered onto the entrance ramp to the freeway, and she didn't see him, she breathed a sigh of relief.

Although a feeling of despair mingled with fear as night fell. She'd left her apartment. Had packed everything she owned in her car and was on the run. She had no idea how to rebuild her life, but her first priority was to escape him.

The protective order she'd filed hadn't mattered to him. He'd ignored it. Had broken in and threatened her. Had promised to make her pay if she ever tried to leave.

Then he'd tied her up and left her naked and alone. His ugly gray eyes had pierced her as he'd told her she needed to think about how to be a good wife.

They weren't married. She'd turned down his proposal. Had made several attempts to break it off with him.

He'd refused to accept that it was over.

When she'd managed to free herself, she'd spent the night in a cheap motel somewhere on the highway, terrified and debating where to go. The police had said they couldn't help her unless he hurt her.

She didn't want to die.

This morning, she'd made a decision. Move to Raleigh where her sister lived. The two of them needed each other. And Tess deserved to know why Reese had cut off communication with her the last few months.

A gust of wind slammed against her vehicle, the windows rattling with the force. A storm was brewing. She had fifteen miles to go.

Her phone dinged with another text. Him again. He'd started calling and texting the minute he'd discovered she was gone.

You'll be sorry for leaving me.

The only thing she was sorry for was ever believing he was a nice man. For signing up for that stupid online dating site.

Her friends said it would be easy. Safe. They were all doing it.

All she had to do was create a profile. Post some pictures. Swipe if she liked someone.

Meet in a public place. Like a coffee shop.

And she had.

He'd been so charming in the beginning. Almost shy. Quiet. Like a gentle giant, he'd complimented her and wined and dined her. She'd lost her mother the year before and had still been grieving. He'd offered a shoulder to cry on. Had understood the reason she'd dropped out of college to work for a while.

He'd promised to take care of her.

She hadn't known that meant isolating her from friends and family and trying to control her.

Finally, she reached the exit for Raleigh. She considered giving her sister a heads-up she was on her way, but figured she needed to explain in person. Perspiration beaded on her neck as she took the exit ramp and veered onto the side street leading to her sister's little house. Tess was an artist and worked at a coffee bar near the downtown area.

But she chose to live outside the city limits for the privacy. She said the countryside inspired her creativity.

The ten miles to her house seemed like an eternity, but Reese grew more relaxed as she approached. She'd missed her sister these last few months. Needed her now.

But as she rounded the corner, she spotted smoke in the air. Thick plumes drifted up into the clouds and swirled in a blinding haze of gray.

She punched the accelerator and sped the next mile. Just as she'd feared, her sister's house was on fire.

Terror pulsed through her as she screeched to a stop. She punched in 9-1-1 and asked for help, then threw the car door open and hit the ground running. Flames had caught the roof and seemed to be coming from the back room. Tess's studio.

The chemicals she used to paint and clean her brushes were there. Oh, God…

The wind howled as she ran toward the house. Maybe her sister wasn't here. Although her little Toyota was in the drive.

Reese pushed the front door open and screamed, "Tess!" She called her name over and over as she raced through the small bungalow. Tess wasn't in the living room or kitchen.

Smoke billowed everywhere. Wood crackled and popped from the back rooms. She coughed and covered her mouth with her scarf but refused to turn back.

Heat scalded her as she inched down the hallway. The guest room was empty but filled with smoke. Tess's bedroom…so much smoke she could barely see inside.

She ducked into the room anyway. But Tess wasn't in there.

Terror clawed at her. The studio.

Flames were starting to lick the edge of the door-way.

"Tess!" She blinked and peered inside. Flames crept

up the wall. Her sister's canvases were on fire, the beautiful colors of paint dripping like blood. Smoke and fire consumed the shelves of art supplies.

Then she saw her sister. On the floor. Not moving.

Screaming her name again, she raced toward her. Fire ate at the window curtains. A piece of burning wood splintered from the shelf and pelted her. Flames licked at her shirt, but she threw the splintered wood aside and beat at the flames. She knelt and shook her sister. Tess was unconscious.

Please, dear God, let her be alive.

Fear driving her, she grabbed her sister's arms and began to drag her from the room. Sweat poured down her face and neck. Something shattered. The floor was growing hot, the fire spreading. She had to hurry.

She yanked and pulled with all her might, hauling her sister through the living room to the front door. A siren wailed in the distance. Lights twirled and glittered across the dark sky.

She pulled Tess onto the porch then down the steps and dragged her across the grass to a nearby tree. Then she dropped to the ground and shook her.

"Tess, honey, hang in there!" She felt for a pulse, but nothing. Seconds ticked by. A fire engine roared into the driveway. Firefighters jumped from the fire engine and sprang into action.

She shouted for help. "My sister. She's not breathing!"

One of the firemen ran over, his face etched in worry as he stooped down and pressed two fingers to her sister's neck.

A second later, he shook his head.

"No…" She refused to give up. She shoved him aside and started chest compressions. Understanding on his face, he murmured that he'd take over.

She stared in shock as he worked to try to save her sister. But as he performed CPR, she spotted ligature marks around Tess's neck. Saw the imprint of someone's fingers. A man's.

Her hand flew to her own throat. Robert had choked her once. Had left marks like those.

His threats taunted her. *You'll be sorry.*

An ambulance careened up. Medics hopped out and raced to help. Firefighters rolled out hoses, dousing the flames with water. The roof collapsed.

The medic traded a look with the firefighter. "It's been too long," he murmured.

The medic checked Tess's pulse. Her heart. Then his look turned to sympathy. "I'm sorry."

Reese shook her head in denial. Tears leaked from her eyes and dripped down her chin. She dragged her sister into her arms and held her, rocking her and crying as the truth seeped into her consciousness.

Robert had been here. He'd killed her sister to punish her.

Tess, the only person she had left in the world. Her best friend. Her little sister. Gone.

Dead at twenty-six.

And it was all her fault.

Chapter One

Three years later

Firefighter and arson investigator, Griffin, *Griff*, Maverick gritted his teeth. Wildfires were springing up all over the mountains. Some were accidental while others had been set by careless hikers—or, as he suspected in this case, teenagers.

He had to put a stop to it. If only he could catch the little culprits. But so far, they'd evaded the police.

At least there were no casualties at this point. But there was always the chance, especially with March winds roaring through, that one would spread and not only destroy property and the beautiful forests along the Appalachian Trail, but that someone would be injured or die in one of the blazes.

He'd nearly lost a member of his own team today when a tree had cracked and splintered down on top of Barney, trapping him in the midst of a brush fire. His leg had been broken in two places, and he'd had to be airlifted to the hospital. Just in time, too, before the flames had caught his clothing.

The scent of smoke and charred wood clung to

Griff's clothes as he loped inside the bar to join his three brothers for their weekly burger and beer night. Now that Jacob and Fletch were married, occasionally they had to skip a week, but they were all committed to keeping up the tradition and the brotherhood bond. The Maverick men stuck together.

They'd also joined forces to find the person who'd set the hospital fire in Whistler five years ago and killed their father.

Fletch, Jacob and Liam were already seated with a bucket of fries and a pitcher of beer. Recently Fletch, who worked search and rescue with FEMA, had found evidence of a possible suspect living off the grid in the mountains.

Finally.

"You look like hell," Fletch said as Griff slid onto the bar stool.

He felt like, it, too. "No time to go home and change."

"Still no idea who's responsible for these wildfires?" Liam, FBI, asked.

"I wish I did." Griff accepted the mug of beer Liam offered. "Third one in two weeks."

"Happens every year," Jacob, sheriff of Whistler, commented.

Liam dug a fry into the ketchup then popped it in his mouth. "I've been looking for similar instances across North Carolina, but so far no unsolved ones."

"I spoke to the principal at the high school," Jacob interjected. "Asked both the school counselor and principal to alert us if they hear any chatter. Counselor wants to protect the students' privacy, but I emphasized that it's only a matter of time before someone loses his or her life and that will constitute murder. She said the school plans to hold an assembly this week. Maybe you can speak at the school, Griff."

He grimaced. The last thing he wanted to do was talk to a bunch of unruly, rebellious teenagers. He'd been one himself.

Of course, that made him qualified, he guessed.

"I could come along and watch the kids' reactions to see if anyone gets nervous," Jacob suggested.

Griff shrugged. "It's worth a shot." He took a swig of his beer. "Where are you on that forensics Fletch found in the cave in the mountains?"

Liam shifted. "Like I said before, the prints match Barry Inman's."

Inman had come unhinged after his wife died in the ER at the hospital. He'd filed a lawsuit, but it had been thrown out the day before the fire. He'd threatened revenge.

Liam plucked another fry from the bucket. "I spoke to his brother, but he hasn't talked to him in years. Said he disappeared after the fire and none of the family has heard from him."

"How about the wife's family?" Griff asked.

"According to the wife's mother, Barry completely lost it after his wife's death. Apparently, he'd been laid off from work and they were having financial problems before she got sick. Mother didn't believe the hospital was negligent and urged him to drop the case, but she claimed he was crazed and obsessed with the idea of making the establishment pay."

"He could be our perp," Jacob commented.

Liam nodded. "When we find him, we'll bring him in for questioning."

"I've been staking out the area where he'd holed up in my spare time and conducting routine searches for him," Fletch admitted.

Anxiety tightened Griff's shoulders. The fire five years ago had taken multiple lives and destroyed families. Cora Reeves's baby had been kidnapped in the chaos, although recently Jacob had found the missing little girl and reunited her with her mother. Then he'd married Cora and made the child his stepdaughter.

"We'll keep working it," Liam said, and they all murmured agreement.

They spent the next hour catching up on sports and other work news. Just as he was finishing his burger, Griff's phone buzzed. Jacob's phone rang, as well.

They answered at the same time.

"9-1-1 report. Fire in progress," his captain told Griff over the phone. "Texting you the address now." Griff stood as the message appeared on his screen. The address—Joy Norris's apartment above the nail salon she owned. Damn. He hoped Joy wasn't there. He'd dated her a few times, but learned she'd lied about her divorce being final. Griff didn't tolerate lies, so he'd broken it off.

"Be right there."

"I'm on my way," Jacob said, tossing some cash on the table.

Griff added a twenty to the pile, and he and Jacob headed to the exit.

Not knowing how long they'd be at the scene, they drove separately. Jacob flipped on his siren and led the way. A mile from the salon, Griff spotted the smoke.

The other storefronts nearby looked safe—for now. But the blaze had to be contained.

Jacob's tires squealed as he veered onto the curb. Griff pulled in behind him, then jumped out and met the crew from his firehouse by the truck. He quickly yanked on his gear.

Jacob caught his arm before he went inside. Déjà vu of the blaze where they'd lost their father struck him. One look at Jacob, and he realized his brother was reliving that horrible day, too.

"Careful, bro." Jacob's eyes darkened. "You're gonna be an uncle."

"I'm always careful." Then Jacob's words registered, and he gave his brother a hug. "Congrats, man. You'll be a great father just like Dad was." He was already a great stepfather.

Emotions clogged Griff's throat, but he swallowed them back and headed into the burning building.

REESE TAGGART HAD been living a lie for the past three years. Hiding out from life. Hiding out from her real identity.

Hiding out from *him*.

Darkness surrounded her. Her sister had been the one who'd seen the colors. Tess had used soft, muted shades of blue and green and vibrant reds and oranges in her landscapes.

When she died, the colors faded for Reese. Now the world was nothing but an ugly brown like the brittle ashes of her sister's house when it had burned to the ground.

She pounded the punching bag, giving it a sharp

right hook, then swung around, lifted her leg and kicked it with all her force. Perspiration beaded on her neck as she went another round, releasing her rage and frustration on the bag as if it was the demon who'd forced her to give up her life and go on the run.

The police had said they'd protect her. They'd looked for her sister's killer. Issued an APB and BOLO and utilized every other kind of official method of tracking down Robert Bouldercrest possible. But he had virtually disappeared.

No credit cards had shown up, no driver's license in another state, no banking information, no posts on social media.

Just like her, he'd changed his name and started over somewhere else.

Had he already found another obsession? Or was he still looking for her?

She slammed her foot into the bag again, then spun her body into a one-eighty turn and gave it a hard-left jab.

"Looking good there, Ginny."

Virginia Bagwell—Ginny—was the name she'd assumed. This gym rat wanted to get personal. Just like Ian Phelps, her instructor at the shooting range, did.

Not going to happen. She'd never trust another man again.

Ian was a former cop and still had friends on the force. She'd actually considered asking him for help once. But too many bad memories had surfaced. Cops who hadn't believed Robert was the monster she claimed him to be. Cops who hinted that she'd asked for what had happened to her.

Besides, Ian had friends who might become curious about her and unearth her real identity. She couldn't let that happen.

No one would find out the truth, not until Robert was behind bars.

Or dead.

She preferred the latter. In fact, she'd been training for it.

The gym rat sauntered over to her, mopping his sweaty face with a towel. "How about we grab a drink when you're finished?" His killer smile and toned body had charmed the pants off half the women who belonged to this gym. She'd watched them croon over him, choose machines beside him to nab his attention. Even request personal training sessions.

Once he conquered them, he dropped them like hot potatoes.

But he was persistent, and if she ignored him, he'd simply go for the chase. That was the kind of guy he was.

"Can't. Got a date," she lied.

"I didn't know you were seeing anyone."

"Yeah. Long time now."

She turned her back to him and punched the bag again, knowing her knuckles would probably be bruised and bloody when she finished. Even the gloves didn't protect her when she unleashed her rage. But she wanted to be strong. Had to be.

If Robert came after her again, she'd be ready.

"Joy!" Griff twisted the doorknob and the door swung open. Heat blasted him, the fire already eating the floor and crawling along the worn carpet. "Joy!"

Flames danced in the kitchen and living area. He maneuvered through the hallway, dodging the flames as he searched the apartment. Living room empty. No one in the bathroom.

"Joy!" He darted through the doorway which was surrounded by flames and spotted Joy on the floor by the bed. Fire engulfed the curtains and crawled around the windowsill.

His heart hammered as he dove through a fiery patch and bent to scoop her up in his arms. She was so still and lifeless that he didn't think she was breathing. Flames nipped at his heels as he carried her through the house, down the steps and outside.

The building crashed and exploded as he rushed to escape. It was chaos outside. More police had arrived. Neighbors, business owners and curiosity seekers had gathered to watch. Sirens and lights twirled against the night sky. Fire hissed and wood crackled. The windows blew, glass shattering and spraying.

One of the medics met him, and Griff eased Joy's body onto the stretcher. Her hair had started to singe. Smoke and soot stained her clothes and limbs.

At least he'd rescued her before the fire had gotten her.

The medic checked Joy's pulse. Then her heart.

His own hammered as the medic murmured that she was gone.

Jacob jogged over to them, his face worried. "Griff?"

He spoke through gritted teeth, "She was already dead when I went inside."

Jacob grimaced. "No one else in there?"

"It's clear."

"How did the fire start?" Jacob asked. "Did you smell gas or an accelerant?"

"Don't know yet," Griff said. "I'll have to wait until it dies out and cools down before I can go in. But if someone had set the salon on fire, the chemicals and acetone in that salon would have been a natural accelerant." He hesitated. "Although why would someone want to burn down the nail salon?"

Jacob shrugged. "We'll look into that. Maybe she was in financial trouble and wanted the insurance money."

Griff mulled over that possibility. He didn't remember Joy having financial problems, but small businesses were a tough go. Hers could be suffering.

"Does she have family to notify?" Jacob asked.

"No, just the ex."

A pinched look marred Jacob's face as he examined Joy's body more closely. "Look at that." Jacob pointed out bruises on Joy's neck.

Griff's blood went cold. "Dammit, this was no accident. She was murdered." And the fire had been set to cover it up.

Two hours later

GINNY CHECKED OVER her shoulder as she unlocked the door to her Asheville apartment. She'd driven a different route home from the gym today and kept alert. Varying her routine had become a necessity for survival.

Stalkers studied behavior patterns. Robert had certainly learned hers. Even after she'd tried to break it

off with him, he'd watched her from the shadows. He'd
known where she shopped, ate, the trails she liked to
jog, her friends, even the drugstore she frequented.
She'd even caught him combing through her trash.

She'd never considered he'd hurt Tess, but she'd
learned her lesson. Since her sister died, she hadn't
allowed herself to get close to anyone.

She couldn't live with another person's death on
her conscience.

She twisted the main lock on the door as she entered the foyer, then the two dead bolts. Still, she kept
one hand on the .22 in her pocket as she searched the
rooms. Satisfied no one was inside, she stowed her
pistol in the drawer by the sofa, then poured herself a
whiskey and carried it to the table.

She opened her laptop and once again searched the
internet and social media, hoping to find a picture of
Robert somewhere. He'd hunted her like a dog that
last month.

It was time he learned what it felt like to be hunted.

An hour later, her muscles ached from fatigue, and
she flipped on the TV to watch the evening news just
as she did each night. The weather report aired, then
national news, then a special breaking story.

A fire in Whistler, NC.

She clutched her glass with a white-knuckled grip
as the reporter interviewed Sheriff Jacob Maverick. He
stood in front of a burning building, flames lighting
up the sky. The street was chaotic, emergency lights
twirling.

"Sheriff, can you tell us what happened here tonight?" the reporter asked.

Beads of sweat trickled down the side of the sheriff's face. "We're on the scene of a fire at Joy's Nail Salon.

"Although our local fire station responded immediately, the chemicals inside the salon caused the blaze to spread quickly. At this point, workers are trying to contain the blaze and keep it from spreading to neighboring businesses."

The camera panned to an ambulance, a doctor standing with the medics and a tall broad-shouldered fireman.

"What about the owner?" the reporter asked. "Was she inside the salon when it caught fire? Were there injuries? Casualties?"

The sheriff shifted. "Unfortunately, the owner of the shop, Joy Norris, was dead when we arrived."

A photograph of the woman flashed on the screen. "If anyone has information regarding her death or the fire tonight, please contact my office."

The number for Whistler's sheriff's department appeared, but the numbers blurred in Ginny's mind as her gaze latched on to the woman.

Joy Norris had shoulder-length auburn hair. Green eyes. A heart shaped face. And ivory skin.

Ginny's chest constricted. She was Robert's type. And a dead ringer for Ginny herself.

Chapter Two

The next morning, Ginny mentally reviewed the news report on the Whistler fire as she drove toward the small mountain town.

Joy Norris's death had been ruled a homicide. The sheriff hadn't revealed details, but she was dead before the fire started. They hadn't reported cause of death though, which raised her suspicions.

She thumped her fingers on her thigh. Was she trying to make a connection where there wasn't one?

Determined to find out if her suspicions had merit, she followed the winding mountain road to Griffin Maverick's cabin. She'd decided to approach the arson investigator instead of the sheriff. Although he was the sheriff's brother, at least he wasn't law enforcement.

Winter was still hanging on, the wind roaring, the trees bare of leaves. As she parked in front of the rustic log cabin, she took a second to admire its sprawling front porch. It looked post card picturesque, much like the little town that was nestled amongst the Appalachian Mountains.

The wind rolled off the mountain, creating a chill in the air. Yet the sound of the river thrashing over rocks drifting from the property in back added a calmness to the breathtaking natural beauty.

She rubbed her hands up and down her arms as she climbed the porch steps, then knocked. After a minute, when she didn't hear sounds inside, she rang the doorbell, mentally bracing herself. She'd planned her cover story on the drive. A way to finagle information without revealing her identity or her past or having to rely on the sheriff.

She'd put all her faith in the law before, but they'd let her down from day one. Two years ago, she'd chased a similar lead/story and confided in a detective working the case in Charlotte. But he'd only paid her lip service. Then he'd accepted a bribe from Robert to find out where she was.

She'd barely escaped alive and had been forced to change her name again. Thank God for the underground society who helped women like her.

Like her. She'd thought she was strong and independent. Had never dreamed she'd be in this situation. Had had the ridiculous misbelief that domestic violence and stalking only happened to weak women.

She was wrong.

Crazies came in all sizes and styles, some of them cunning and handsome and so manipulative they knew exactly how to get in the mind of their victims and find their weaknesses. They preyed on women, women who were oblivious to the fact they were being targeted.

Her downfall had been trusting others.

No more.

She took a deep breath, fluffed her layered bob, which was now a soft black instead of auburn, and adjusted the dark blue blazer she'd picked up at the thrift store.

Finally, she heard a noise inside. Footsteps.

She peered through the window and spotted Griffin Maverick shuffling toward the front door. His hair looked mussed, and he ran a hand over his eyes as if he'd just woken up.

She should have called. But she'd suspected he might deny her an interview. And if Robert had set the fire the night before, she wanted to know.

He swung the door open, blinking at the morning sunlight with a frown. Dear heavens, he was a handsome man. Tall, built like a linebacker, a broad face, shadow of a beard, dark hair, deep brown eyes with flecks of gold.

"I'm sorry," she sputtered, thrown by her reaction to him. Of course, any red-blooded female would be shaken by his raw masculinity. But she didn't allow herself to fantasize that there might be a good man beneath the package.

Not anymore.

"Sorry?" he said his voice gruff. "What, are you lost or something?"

She shook her head, willing her voice to be steady and not reveal the fact that she was about to feed him a big fat lie.

Protecting herself and getting revenge were all that mattered. If she had to use this man to do that, then let the lies begin.

GRIFF STARED AT the woman in confusion. Strange, beautiful females didn't just show up at his door early in the morning, not out here.

Hell, he'd been up half the night working the crime scene and felt as scruffy as he must look.

She lifted a dainty chin. "My name is Virginia—Ginny—Bagwell," she said in a voice that sounded almost angelic. Or hell, maybe he was still asleep and dreaming. In deep REM.

"I'm an investigative journalist," she continued. "I'm writing a special series on arson, specifically arsonists and their motives, and would like to interview you for my piece."

Griff narrowed his eyes. "I'm sorry, but I've been up half the night working. Why don't you contact my firehouse and talk to the captain? He has people who handle media coverage." Griff hated the press. Being in the spotlight. Last night he'd left Jacob to handle the reporter at the salon so he could concentrate on his job.

"Please," Ginny said with a soft smile that probably disarmed most men. Or had them falling at her pretty feet. And he bet they were pretty and girly although you wouldn't know it from the plain black flat shoes she wore. They were as nondescript as the black sedan she was driving.

"I did my research," she went on. "I know how well respected you are, that you're a leader among your team. I saw the story about the fire last night. You worked it."

Griff shifted. "So did other members at my station."

She clamped her teeth over her bottom lip, a lip so plump and ripe that for a moment Griff's body stirred with desire.

Good grief. What was wrong with him?

Sleep deprivation. That was all.

She fidgeted with the button on her jacket. "I'm sorry for bothering you. You obviously were up late. Maybe I could buy you a cup of coffee later? Or breakfast? How about it, Mr. Maverick?"

She was persistent.

"Who did you say you work for? A paper? Magazine?" Griff asked.

A second of hesitation, then she breathed out. "I'm not with anyone at the moment. I'm trying to get an in at a TV network, and the only way to do that is to come up with a good story."

"You can get information on arsonists' motives on the internet," he said, sensing she was trouble.

"I don't want simple rote facts," she said. "I want the real story from someone who's worked fires, who knows arson, who's been in the head of a fire starter and understands his actions."

He leaned against the doorframe. "Understanding means I sympathize with the arsonist, and I don't. But I do recognize their motives. Human nature makes us want to know why people do the things they do, especially actions that hurt others. And knowing those motives can lead to finding the culprits."

"That's exactly what I'm talking about," she said. "Please meet me for coffee later."

She extended a business card with her name and phone number in black and white. "I'm going to book a room at the local inn. Just let me know when you're ready to talk."

Their fingers brushed as he accepted the card, and the sleeve of her jacket rode up slightly. Just enough to reveal a scar on the underside of her wrist. Puckered red skin. Raw looking.

A burn scar.

His pulse jumped. Ginny Bagwell might be researching a story, but she was holding something back. This was personal to her.

She'd come to him because she'd researched him. That roused his curiosity.

"All right, I'll call you after I get some sleep," he said, hoping a couple hours of z's would make her look less sexy when he talked to her.

Either way, he'd find out what she was up to.

GINNY STRUGGLED TO calm her raging nerves as she drove through the small town of Whistler. Nestled in the mountains only a couple of hours from Asheville, it looked like a quaint little village with its gift shops, handmade quilt store and signs for boiled peanuts and homemade fudge. The area catered to campers, hikers, white-water rafting, canoeing and skiing in the winter.

She'd read everything she could find on the town the night before. Five years ago, a terrible fire had destroyed the local hospital, caused several casualties and cost the Maverick brothers their father's life.

Griff knew what it was like to lose a loved one. Her heart went out to him. Yet that fact could give them common ground.

Reminding herself to stay alert in case Robert was in Whistler, she scanned the streets as she drove and the parking lot of the Whistler Inn when she pulled into the drive. Set against the backdrop of the sharp ridges and hills beyond, it looked almost ethereal. Not that she could relax and enjoy it while she stayed here.

Not with her sister's killer still on the loose.

She retrieved her overnight bag from the trunk of her rental car and started up the cobblestone walkway to the front door of the inn. The hair on the back of her neck prickled, and she turned and scanned the street again.

Robert couldn't know she was here. Could he?

No. She'd been careful. Rented a car using her fake ID so it couldn't be traced back to Reese Taggart. Her hair was a different color now and shorter. Thanks to colored contacts, her green eyes were blue.

Reminding herself that she was here to find him, and that she'd trained for the moment, she slipped inside the inn. The woman behind the guest-services desk smiled and offered her the room she called The Sunflower Room. Ginny expected it to be painted bright yellow, but it was white with muted shades of green and coral, and fresh sunflowers in a vase on the desk.

The room was so bright and cheery that it looked at odds with the reason she'd come. But it reminded her of a happier time when she and her sister had dreamed about their futures together.

Tess had lost her future because of her.

Tears blurred her eyes. Some days she made it through without succumbing to the overwhelming anguish. Other days, the grief came out of nowhere and hit her so hard it stole her breath.

It was the little things that triggered the memories and made her choke up with emotions and regret.

Tess's favorite ice cream was mint chocolate chip. On her birthday, Ginny ordered a cone of it to honor Tess, but halfway through she'd started bawling like a baby. Another time she'd heard her sister's favorite song in a coffee shop, and she'd had to leave.

She swiped at the tears and forced herself to focus on her mission. Hopefully Griffin Maverick would call her.

If not, she'd find another way to see if the death of the woman in the nail-salon fire was connected to Robert.

She settled her suitcase on the luggage rack, then set her laptop on the desk. Her muscles ached from tension and tossing and turning all night. The dead woman's face taunted her in her sleep. Joy looked so much like she had three years ago that Ginny felt like she was looking in the mirror.

If she'd never gotten involved with Robert, Tess would still be alive.

And if she'd stopped Robert a long time ago, he couldn't have hurt anyone else, like Joy.

She grabbed a bottle of water from the gift basket on the corner table, uncapped it and took a long drink as she sank into the chair and booted up her computer.

This trip to Whistler might not turn up anything on Robert. Joy Norris's murder might be unrelated to Tess's.

But that picture, Joy's looks… She had to know for sure if she was another victim of Robert's.

She spent the next hour combing the internet for pictures or any mention of Robert Bouldercrest. She checked local news reports and social media, trolling through random photographs people had posted.

But she found nothing.

Determined to explore every avenue, she decided to search online dating sites again. She'd met Robert on a site called Meet Your Mate and went there first in case he stuck to a pattern.

She created a new profile under the name June Embers and found a stock photo to use. She answered the questions in a similar vein as she had when she'd created her first profile.

If Robert had been attracted to quiet, shy journalism student Reese Taggart who lived alone and had just lost her mother, he might fall for bookstore owner June who'd grown up in foster care and wanted to get married and make a family of her own. She posted the profile, then added it to several other dating and singles sites.

Robert liked playing the savior, the knight riding in to save the lonely damsel. Like June.

And he *had* been chivalrous. Affectionate. Romantic.

Until he'd turned into a monster.

THREE HOURS LATER, Griff rolled from bed, still foggy from sleep. He felt as if he was in a phantasmagoric state, where real images and imagined ones blurred together. Had he been so exhausted he'd dreamed that beautiful woman had shown up at his door this morning?

His phone dinged with a text as he stumbled into the kitchen. Jacob.

One p.m. Meet at ME's office for results of Joy Norris's autopsy.

Griff sent a return text: See you there.

He started past the breakfast island to make coffee when he spotted the business card Ginny had left. So, he hadn't imagined her.

He filled the coffee carafe with water and poured it into the coffee maker, inserted a filter filled with his favorite ground beans, then punched the start button. While the rich, dark coffee brewed, he picked up the card, turned it over between his fingers and studied it. Simple office stationery. Classic design.

The name Virginia (Ginny) Bagwell was scrawled in italics with the title investigative journalist printed below her name along with a phone number and address in Asheville.

He tapped the card between his fingers, his curiosity piqued. How had she gotten that scar? Why was this story important enough to travel to Whistler and knock on his door?

His pulse jumped as a random thought struck him. Could she possibly know something about the fire from five years ago?

The scar…could she have been at the hospital that day?

Chapter Three

The scent of chicory filled the air, and Griff poured himself a cup of coffee, carried it to his computer then sat down and retrieved the file he, Jacob, Liam and Fletch had compiled over the past five years. He plugged in the name Virginia (Ginny) Bagwell and ran a search to see if her name was listed as one of the victims in the Whistler Hospital fire, or if she'd lived in town at the time.

Nothing popped.

Even more curious than before, he snagged his cell phone and pressed the number on the business card. He had a couple of hours before meeting the ME and Jacob.

She answered on the third ring. "Hi. I didn't know if you'd call, Mr. Maverick."

He hadn't known if he would either.

"It's Griff. I can do a late breakfast at eleven at Mitzi's Café in the town square." The young woman had just opened, and he'd heard the food was good. She was not only attractive, but she made a mean stack of hotcakes with fresh blueberries and cream. He did have a sweet tooth.

"I'll be there."

He hung up, then headed to the shower. While she probed him for information about arsonists, he'd find out what she was hiding.

GINNY CHECKED TO make sure her auburn roots weren't bleeding through before walking to the café. Outside, the sun was battling its way through dark clouds that hinted at rain, and the wind tossed debris through the air.

She checked over her shoulder a dozen times, keeping a lookout as she crossed the street and bypassed the mercantile and arts-and-crafts store.

Hunching her shoulders against the wind, she hurried past a dark gray SUV, averting her face until she reached the awning of The Brew, the coffee shop on the corner. She ducked beneath it, slipping into the shadows, then pulled her binoculars and aimed them at the vehicle.

Was Robert inside?

She hovered there for several seconds, watching. Finally, the man opened the door and stepped from the SUV.

Not Robert. This man was heavyset, bearded, with graying hair.

Relief surged through her, and she rushed down the sidewalk to the café.

Mitzi's looked like a throwback to the Wild West with its saloon door and red-checked tablecloths. Country music wafted through the speakers, and the sound of voices, laughter and dishes clanging filled the dining area.

She stopped at the hostess stand and told the young girl she was meeting someone, then asked for the booth in the rear. She always faced the door, never put her back to an entry point. She also scanned the room for a rear exit in case she needed to make a hasty escape.

Once seated, she ordered coffee and checked her phone, searching for updates on the story about the fire. Nothing new.

Footsteps sounded, and she looked up and saw Griff approaching. His big body seemed to take up all the space, stirring a myriad of emotions inside her. Fear, because he was big and muscled and strong. Desire, because he was handsome as sin.

Just the kind of men she avoided. She glanced at the scar on her wrist as a reminder. *Play with fire and you get burned.*

Sometimes you didn't survive.

She had to survive long enough to get revenge for Tess.

GRIFF NARROWED HIS EYES as he claimed the chair across from Ginny. He'd seen her outside on the street. Watched her checking over her shoulder as if she thought someone was following her. Saw her duck beneath the awning, pull out her binoculars and surveil the man in that gray SUV.

What in the hell was she doing?

Was she really here for basic information on arson or was she chasing another story?

She offered him a smile that instantly made his gut tighten. "Thank you for coming."

"Had to eat," he said gruffly.

She nodded and sipped her coffee. The waitress sauntered over and he ordered coffee and the stack of hotcakes with blueberries and whipped cream. She asked for the same except she chose strawberries for her topping.

She wasted no time but jumped in with basic questions about causes of fire.

"Many are accidental," he said, playing along. "Faulty wiring. Someone left a candle burning or dropped a cigarette or left the stove on."

"How about those recent wildfires?"

Their food arrived, and his stomach was growling so he dug in. "Could be campers or hikers not properly extinguishing their campfire. The March winds can whip up embers and spark flames even after the fire has been thought to have been snuffed out."

"Is that what you think is happening?"

He shrugged. "Honestly I think some teens are the cause, but we haven't found a suspect, or suspects." He waved his hand. "This is off the record. Do you understand?"

"I do," she said quietly. "You found an accelerant?"

He nodded. "A couple of packs of matches. Empty beer cans. Evidence of lighter fluid."

"That does sound intentional. Is there a pattern with the timing?"

"Not really. Although two of them started at dusk. Just enough time for kids to get out of school, head to the woods and drink a few beers before their folks got home from work."

He finished off his meal, then sat back and studied her while he sipped his coffee.

"Tell me about pyromaniacs," she said. "They're obsessed with fire, aren't they?"

"True. Some have impulse disorders. They love the thrill of watching the flames burn. But that's more rare."

She licked whipped cream from her lips. "A large percentage of arsonists set fires to cover a crime, don't they?"

Now he sensed they were getting to the heart of the matter. "As a matter of fact, yes. Fire can destroy valuable evidence and make recovering forensics difficult." He paused. "But a fire doesn't totally destroy a body. Specialists can still uncover important forensics and evidence by examining the remains."

"Is that what happened last night at the nail salon? Do you think someone killed Joy Norris then set the salon on fire to cover his tracks?"

He folded his arms. "I can't divulge information in an ongoing investigation."

"But that's what you suspect?" she pressed.

"Is that why you're here?" He narrowed his eyes. "Do you know something about that fire last night or Joy's murder?"

Her eyes widened slightly. "I explained that I'm writing a piece on arson—"

"I'm not buying it," he said. He'd been lied to before by Joy and didn't like it.

She shifted and traced a finger around the rim of her coffee mug. "All right. I'll share if you do."

A frown creased his mouth. "We're still investigating. I'm supposed to meet with the ME and sheriff after breakfast to learn the results of the autopsy." He snagged the bill and gave her a pointed look. "Now your turn."

Her gaze met his for a tension-filled minute. He thought she might answer, but then she yanked her gaze from his as if he'd burned her.

Suddenly a commotion sounded from up front. Loud footsteps. Then a man's voice bellowing.

Griff turned to see what the problem was, his heart hammering when Joy's ex-husband Wayne stalked toward him, hands balled into fists. Griff went still, his jaw clenched as the man grabbed him by the collar of his shirt.

"What the hell did you do to my wife?" Wayne snarled. "First you screw her when we're still married. Then what? She broke it off, so you got mad and killed her?"

GINNY GRIPPED THE chair edge as the man's accusations rang in her head. Griff had slept with this man's wife while she was married to him?

Disappointment filled her. She'd almost confided the truth, at least part of it, to Griff. Had thought that maybe he was a good guy. He saved lives.

But he'd slept with another man's wife.

His body stiffened, and he curled his fingers around the shorter man's hands and pulled free. "Listen to me, Wayne, I did not hurt Joy," he said bluntly. "The minute I learned your divorce wasn't final, I broke it off."

"I don't believe you," the man hissed. "I think you still wanted her, but she told you the two of us were getting back together and you got mad."

"If you two were reconciling, then good for you,"

Griff said, his tone edged with doubt. "Although maybe you're the one who hurt her. Maybe she told you there was no way she'd come back to you, and you snapped."

Ginny fidgeted. If Joy's husband was jealous enough to hurt her, or even kill her, she might be wrong about Robert being in Whistler.

She didn't know whether to be relieved or disappointed. As much as Robert terrified her, she was desperate to get rid of him forever.

"Now, I suggest you go somewhere and cool off," Griff said in a deep voice. "I have a meeting to attend."

He didn't bother to say goodbye to her. He pushed past Joy's husband, strode to the counter to pay the bill, then stormed out the door.

Joy's husband turned and glared at her. "You may think he's some hero, but he's not."

Venom spewed from the man's eyes and tone. Venom that told her he was dangerous. Venom that reminded her of another man who'd shed his charming outer skin to become a snake when she'd crossed him.

Had Joy's husband killed her and set that fire as payback for sleeping with Griff?

Humiliation washed over Griff as he left Mitzi's Café. He hadn't been proud that he'd slept with a married woman, but he hadn't known at the time or it would never have happened. He'd been angry with Joy for lying to him, not for dumping him, but he sure as hell would never have hurt her.

His father had drilled his personal motto into his sons' heads—Respect and Protect, Especially Women and Children. Griff had become a firefighter to honor his father's death.

Wayne Norris, on the other hand, was less than honorable.

He'd driven Joy away with his bullying and drinking. She'd insisted to Griff that she'd never go back to him.

Which meant Wayne was lying about a reconciliation. Maybe about more...

The bastard could have publicly made accusations against Griff to waylay suspicion from himself.

He climbed in his truck and drove to the ME's office, still steaming. His phone buzzed as he parked. The head of the forensics lab.

"Maverick, I have some results," Lieutenant Miller said. "The only accelerant in the building was the acetone and chemicals at the salon."

So, the arsonist was smart. He'd known he hadn't needed additional fuel.

"But tests prove that it wasn't just small amounts spilled here and there. Someone poured acetone throughout the seating area and around the doors and walls."

"He wanted it to spread and spread quickly," Griff surmised.

"Exactly." Lieutenant Miller paused. "Oh, and we also found traces of acetone upstairs in the woman's apartment. Large amounts."

Definitely intentional. "So, there were multiple points of origin?"

"Yes. This guy didn't want to take any chances the fire would die out before it destroyed the whole place."

•

Griff twisted his mouth in thought. "I'll relay that to the sheriff. I'm sure he'll want to look into Joy's financials and her ex's in case of an insurance payout." If Wayne hadn't killed Joy out of spite, he could have done it for money.

Jacob pulled into the parking lot in his police-issued SUV and parked beside Griff.

"Any forensics that might belong to our perp?" Griff asked.

"We're still sorting through," Lieutenant Miller answered. "The fire destroyed most of the place. Add the water and smoke damage to the fact that this business catered to multiple customers daily, and it's a big fat mess."

He agreed to keep Griff updated, and Griff climbed from his vehicle. Jacob did the same, and they walked up the sidewalk together. He filled Jacob in on the forensics report as they entered the building.

"Will definitely look into the ex," Jacob said.

"I just had a run-in with him at Mitzi's Café." Griff explained about the confrontation.

"Sorry about that. I had to inform him of her death last night. But I wanted to wait until the autopsy before I brought him in for questioning."

Griff understood. Jacob would want to be armed with evidence and the ME's report.

"He's a ticking time bomb," Griff said. "Who knows what he's capable of."

"I'll dig up everything I can find on him."

They walked down the hall, then Jacob knocked on the ME's door. Dr. Hammerhead opened it, his thick brows marred into a frown. "Come on in. I'm just about to finish."

The scent of formaldehyde and other chemicals blended with the acrid odor of death. Griff said a silent thank-you to the heavens that Joy's body hadn't been burned. It didn't matter how long he was on the job, he'd never get used to the scent of charred flesh and tissue.

The doctor led them over to the exam table where Joy lay half draped in a cloth. Bins and instruments the ME used lined a sterile stainless steel tray next to the body.

Griff's stomach knotted at the sight of the Y incision on her chest. Her pale skin looked stark white beneath the bright fluorescent light.

Emotions churned through him. Joy might have lied to him, but she hadn't deserved this. She had her whole life ahead of her.

Last night, when he'd carried her from that burning apartment, her skin had looked bluish.

This morning bruises marred her arms. Another one darkened her shoulder.

"I did a full tox screen, and she had alcohol in her system, but no drugs." Dr. Hammerhead lifted one of her eyelids at a time, and Griff swallowed hard.

"Petechial hemorrhaging." He lowered the sheet and gestured toward bruises on Joy's neck. "Official cause of death is asphyxiation due to strangulation."

Just as he and Jacob had surmised. Griff zeroed in on the fingerprints emblazoned on Joy's neck. Large fingerprints.

Wayne's? Or had Joy been involved with another man?

GINNY COULDN'T STAND the wait. She had to know if Joy Norris was strangled. If she'd died at the hands of her husband, Ginny could leave Whistler.

Go back to hiding out.

She was so tired of hiding.

She'd let that jerk ruin her life. Control it for the last three years.

It had to end.

She texted Griff: What did the ME say about Joy Norris's death?

When he didn't respond, she darted outside the cafe. She'd go to the morgue and confront him.

Her senses remained honed as she hurried to cross the street. But just as she stepped off the curb, a car flew around the corner. She jumped back a step, but suddenly someone pushed her from behind.

She lunged forward, hands flailing to stay on her feet, but she plunged into the street, hitting the asphalt on her hands and knees.

Tires screeched and brakes squealed. Then she looked up and saw a car barreling straight toward her.

HE KNEW WHERE Reese was. Had known the moment she'd entered town.

She thought she was so smart. Dying her hair. Changing her name. Skulking in the shadows.

He'd done the same.

But he'd kept tabs on her. Had left her alone for a while and entertained himself with another. Had intended to lull her into a false sense of safety.

She'd come to Whistler to find him. His plan had worked. She must have seen the story about Joy. Joy, who looked so much like Reese that he hadn't been able to help himself.

Joy was gone now though. And he would have Reese again. Nothing would stop him this time.

But he'd have some fun first. He'd toy with her just to watch her squirm and suffer.

He disappeared into the woods by the park, then paused behind a tree to watch the chaos as she rolled sideways on the street to avoid being hit by the car.

Laughter bubbled in his throat. She'd been working out. She looked as if she'd developed muscles beneath the sleeves of that boring suit jacket.

Of course, she'd look better in something more feminine.

His body hardened at the image that played through his head. Reese in a black satin teddy. Red lace panties.

A teddy and panties that wouldn't stay on her long.

Chapter Four

Ginny froze as the car careened toward her. A second later, the screeching of the tires and someone screaming nearby jolted her back into motion, and she rolled sideways. The car swerved to avoid her and jumped the curb, brakes squealing.

Chaos erupted around her. Someone reached down to help her up. A man ordered people to back away from her. Ginny tried to push herself up to stand, but she was shaking all over. Her hands were scraped, bloody and raw. Her knee throbbed where she landed on the pavement.

"Come on, sweetie." A middle-aged woman and her teenage son took her arm and helped her over the curb. Ginny's legs felt weak, her mind racing. Voices rumbled around her. A small crowd had gathered.

The driver of the car, a young woman, leaped from inside and ran toward her. "Oh, my god, are you okay? I…thought you were at the crossing."

She had been. But…someone had pushed her before the traffic light changed. A dizzy spell assaulted her, and she rubbed her temple.

"Someone call 9-1-1," an older man said.

"No." Ginny shook her head and blinked to clear her vision. "I'm fine. No need."

She looked up into the panicked eyes of the driver. She looked shell shocked and terrified. "I hit the brakes when I saw you falling," she said, her voice bordering on hysteria.

"It wasn't your fault," Ginny murmured. "I tripped and fell right in front of you."

"But I could have killed you." The other woman burst into tears, and an elderly woman patted her back to comfort her.

Ginny threw up her hand to stop the chatter. "I'm really fine. It was just an accident, but I'm not hurt." And she sure as hell didn't want to deal with the police.

She rubbed the young driver's arms to calm her. "Look at me, sweetie. You stopped in time. I'm fine now. Really. I was at fault, not you."

Tears blurred the other woman's eyes, and she accepted a handkerchief from a gentleman in a navy suit.

"Please, everyone, go back to your business," Ginny said. "I'm going to my car and clean up now. I'll be fine."

Without waiting for a response, she forced herself to walk toward her car. She'd cross at the other end of the sidewalk. Right now, she wanted to escape the concerned bystanders. They stood talking and whispering for a minute, and Ginny scanned the street across from where she'd fallen. Her ankle throbbed, and she tasted blood. Must have bitten her lip in the fall. Her hands stung and her knee was aching. But she kept walking until she found the next crosswalk. It was practically deserted, and the sign blinked for walkers to cross.

She glanced around her, behind her, to the sides and across the street before she stepped into the crosswalk.

Wind ruffled her hair and sent a chill through her. Or maybe she was chilled from the fall. Except she hadn't simply tripped and fallen.

She pressed the key fob to unlock her car, then slid inside and locked the door. Trembling all over, she dropped her forehead against the steering wheel and dragged in huge gulping breaths. Tears burned her eyes, fear pulsing through her.

She'd felt those hands shove her into the street. Felt someone watching her all day.

And right before she'd fallen, she'd detected the strong scent of a man's cologne. Earthy and musky.

The same scent Robert had worn.

GRIFF AND JACOB drew in deep breaths of fresh air as they stepped outside.

"I'll never get used to the smells in that morgue," Jacob muttered.

Griff raked a hand through his hair. "Me neither."

They paused on the steps, and Jacob turned to Griff. "You said Joy's ex accused you of hurting her because she broke it off. What really happened, Griff?"

He'd been too ashamed that he'd slept with a married woman at the time to confide in his brothers when he discovered Joy's betrayal. "When we met, she told me she was divorced. We dated a few times, nothing serious though. At least not on my part."

"Was she serious?" Jacob asked.

Griff shrugged. "She hinted she wanted a future. But it was an act. One night on the phone, I heard her talking to one of her friends. She said the divorce wasn't final, but she was going to teach Wayne a lesson because he'd cheated on her. She used me to do that."

"That sucks," Jacob said.

"But you're thinking I had motive?"

"Someone else would say that."

Griff's pulse jumped. "Was I mad? Yes. So, I broke it off with her. That was over three months ago."

"Do you have an alibi for last night?"

Anger shot through Griff. "You don't seriously think I'd hurt a woman, do you?"

"Of course not," Jacob said. "But you know I have to eliminate persons of interest and that means anyone involved with Joy or who had a personal beef with her. It's just routine."

The tension in Griff's chest eased slightly. He understood, but he didn't like it. "I was putting out those wildfires all afternoon and evening, up until the time we met for burgers and beer."

Jacob shifted. "I need to bring Wayne in for questioning and find out if he has an alibi."

"Anger at Joy over leaving him could be motive." An idea occurred to Griff. "Or if Joy used me, maybe she used some other man as well."

Jacob's brows shot up. "You're right. I'll speak to her friends and coworkers, find out if she had any other love interests or enemies."

GINNY HAD TO pull herself together. She'd come here looking for Robert.

Maybe she'd found him. Or rather, he'd found her.

The cloying scent of his cologne made her nauseated, stirring memories of him touching her. Hovering over her. Refusing to let her go.

Never again.

Renewing her resolve to make him pay, she lifted her head, inhaled and reached inside the console between the front seats. She removed a pack of sanitizing wipes and cleaned the bloody scrapes on her palms, wiping away streaks of blood and pavement debris.

She glanced at her face in the mirror and checked her appearance. A mess of tangled hair, and tear-streaked cheeks stared back. She dabbed at her face with another wipe, then pulled her compact from her purse and added a thin layer of powder to cover her dark circles and pale skin.

She started the engine and veered onto the street. Using the car's GPS, she followed the directions to the morgue. Maybe she could meet Griff outside and persuade him to talk.

Traffic was slow as she maneuvered through town, checking the side streets and alleys at every turn, and peering at pedestrians and bystanders as she passed the park. A black sedan caught her eye, and she squinted to see through the windows, but the dark tinted glass made it impossible to distinguish the person inside.

Rain clouds gathered above, threatening a spring storm as she approached the morgue. She slowed as the facility came into view. Griff stood hunched in his jacket on the front steps with his brother the sheriff. She swung her car into the parking lot across the street, hoping they didn't see her, and waited for the men to part ways.

They looked serious, deep in conversation, almost

tense with one another. What had they learned from the ME? Had they recovered Joy's computer or phone?

She wished she could search the woman's apartment, but that had burned down in the fire. The sheriff shifted, then patted Griff on the shoulder, turned and walked to his squad car. Griff remained still for a moment, staring at the street, his brows furrowed.

Maybe he was more upset about her death than he'd admitted. If he was in love with Joy, and he discovered Robert had killed her, Griff might blame *her* if he knew the truth about her relationship with him.

All the more reason to keep quiet about her reason for being here until she knew for certain Robert was responsible for Joy's death.

The wind ruffled Griff's thick hair, giving him a rakish look that reminded her men were dangerous. Good looks didn't matter and could be deceiving. What did she know about Griff Maverick anyway? Just that he was a fireman and ran into burning buildings on the job.

He could be a totally different person in his personal life.

Just like Robert had been.

Robert's polished clothes, bulging wallet and slick smile had worked well for him as an investor. He'd certainly sold himself to her. Took her on expensive dates, to lavish dinners, showered her with romantic gifts.

Then he'd thought he owned her.

When she'd finally balked at his possessiveness, his true colors had surfaced.

Griff shaded his eyes with one hand and scanned

the street, and she ducked low in the seat. Had he noticed her?

She held her breath for a minute, then raised her head just enough to glance through the window. He was gone.

Pulse hammering, she gripped the steering wheel and scanned the sidewalk. Where was he? Not in the road, not crossing to her.

A shadow of movement caught her eye, and she spotted him several hundred feet away.

His hands were jammed in the pockets of his leather bomber jacket, his posture tense. When he reached a black pickup truck, he climbed in, started the engine and backed from the parking space.

Ginny started her car and veered from the parking lot, then drove slowly, remaining a car length behind, hoping he wouldn't spot her on his tail.

GRIFF'S MIND REPLAYED his relationship with Joy as he headed back toward his place. She'd been sweet at first, had been friendly at the town council business meeting. She'd just moved to Whistler and was excited about opening her salon. Said she was divorced and starting fresh.

She'd seemed intelligent, independent and was easy on the eyes. He'd taken her to dinner one night and they'd had a few drinks, then she'd asked him back to her apartment. Coming off several days of work, and at the time frustrated with no leads in the hospital fire as he faced the impending anniversary of his father's death, he'd been feeling down and…lonely. Having a pretty woman come on to him had been flattering, and he'd climbed in her bed.

They'd gotten together a couple more times, but soon he'd sensed she wasn't the woman she pretended to be. Then he'd discovered she was still married, and he'd called it quits immediately.

He didn't fool around with married women. And he didn't tolerate lies.

She was both married and a liar.

He swung onto the road leading toward the town square. Maybe he'd ask around town for word about Joy's love life. Perhaps she'd used someone else as she had him, and that man hadn't taken it well. He could always check the bar she frequented.

He glanced in his rearview mirror and frowned. Two cars back, he spotted Ginny Bagwell's little black sedan. Was she following him?

Curious, he made a sharp right turn and sped up, checking the mirror again. She turned and accelerated. If she was following him, she was a damn amateur. Irritated that she thought he wouldn't notice, he drove a couple more miles, then made another turn. She was close behind.

Why the hell was she so determined to talk to him? If she wanted information about Joy's murder, she should go straight to Jacob instead of him.

That baffled him. So did the fact that she'd asked specifically about Joy's death.

Deciding he'd had enough deception to last a lifetime, he swung into a parking spot in front of town hall. She parked two cars down.

Griff slid from his truck and stalked toward her.

When he reached the sedan, he rapped on the window. She hit the automatic button to lower it, then looked up at him with a doe-like expression.

"Griff, funny we meet again," she said feigning surprise as if this was a coincidence.

"It's not funny at all," he growled. "I made you way back there." He folded his arms and glared down at her. "Now, why in the hell are you following me?"

She lifted her chin. "I told you I want a story. I texted you and asked about Joy Norris's COD, but you didn't answer. Was she strangled?"

The sense that she was hiding something intensified. "Why don't you go to the sheriff? Why ask me?"

"Was she strangled?" A hint of desperation laced her tone that roused his curiosity even more.

"Yes," Griff said. "How did you know?"

Her face paled, but she squared her shoulders. "I didn't. It was just a guess."

Griff studied her. Something about her was off…

He leaned against the window, his gaze meeting hers with a warning look. "Listen to me. If you know something about Joy's murder, you'd better come clean. Right now, all we have is her ex. If he's innocent, we've got nothing."

She jerked her gaze from his and stared at her hands which were clenching the steering wheel in a white-knuckled grip. "I… I'm here researching a story," she said again. "I didn't even know Joy."

Maybe so. But she was holding back something.

"If you're scared or something else is going on, I'll go with you to talk to my brother," he offered.

She clamped her teeth over her bottom lip and shook her head. "I have to go. Sorry for disturbing you."

"Just tell me—"

"I won't bother you again. I'll get the information on my own." The window slid up, then she started the engine, backed from the space and drove away.

Just what the hell was she planning? A single woman asking questions about a murder could be dangerous. Didn't she know that?

Chapter Five

Ginny silently chided herself as she drove away. She couldn't allow another man to intimidate her. But Griff Maverick had done just that.

She would just have to do what she'd said. Investigate on her own. Find another way to determine if Joy had been dating Robert.

After deciding to start by chatting up Mitzi at the café, she drove to the quaint little spot, parked and scanned the property before she went inside. Just because she didn't see Robert didn't mean he wasn't lurking around.

Watching her. Trying to unnerve her.

He'd done that before when she'd first left him. When his more subtle pleas and promises to win her back had failed, he'd started stalking her. Showing up in random places. Outside the coffee shop she liked to go to in the mornings. At the library when she'd decided to study and go back to college. At the restaurant where she'd worked part-time to pay for the room she'd rented in the rear.

Sometimes he'd simply sit and watch. Other times he'd leave her notes, reminding her that she was his. Twice she'd gone back to the apartment and realized he'd been inside.

He'd left a gift for her on the bed. Flowers. Perfume. A silk teddy he wanted her to wear.

That same cloying cologne he wore had lingered in the air, suffocating and nauseating.

She inhaled to ward off her nerves and entered the café. The scent of coffee and apple pie wafted toward her. Mitzi stood behind the counter pouring coffee into two mugs for an elderly man and woman. The couple carried the mugs to a corner table and huddled together as if they were newlyweds.

Ginny's heart gave a pang. At one time she'd dreamed of love and happily-ever-after. Then Tess had been taken from her. Tess who would never have a chance to love or be loved or hold her own baby in her arms. Tess whose art brightened the world. A world now void of color without her in it.

Ginny slid onto the bar stool and forced a friendly smile toward Mitzi. The young woman's blond hair accentuated her narrow face and was twisted into a claw clip on top of her head. She was probably mid-twenties, looked friendly and easygoing as she managed the various orders tossed at her.

"What can I get you?" Mitzi asked as she handed off a cappuccino to the waitress to deliver to another table.

"Just plain coffee," Ginny said. Her stomach couldn't handle anything richer today, not after the scent of that cologne.

Mitzi arched a brow in question as she slid a steaming mug toward her. "You're the woman who was here with Griff earlier, aren't you?"

Ginny drizzled honey into her coffee. "Yes, I'm an investigative journalist researching a story on arsonists.

I heard about the fire at the nail salon and was hoping he could add some insight."

Mitzi rearranged the condiments on the bar. "Then you're not from around here?"

"No, and I don't intend to stay," Ginny said, deciding to let the woman know she wasn't a threat in case Mitzi was interested in Griff. "I'll be leaving as soon as I finish my story." She stirred her coffee. "By the way, did you know the owner of the salon?"

Mitzi's lips pinched into a frown, and she propped her elbows on the bar. At this time of the day, the place was virtually empty. Still, Mitzi spoke in a conspiratorial whisper. "We met, but I didn't think much of her. I heard she'd used Griff and that she went through men like some women change their shoes."

"Really?" Ginny absorbed that tidbit. "Do you recall seeing her with anyone specific?"

Mitzi twisted her mouth in thought. "A couple of times she came in with this really handsome fellow. Said he was an investment banker who helped her secure the loan for her salon."

"What did he look like?" Ginny asked.

"Late thirties, brown hair, neatly trimmed, well dressed. He seemed really flirty with her, so I wondered if there was more to their relationship than business."

"Do you recall his name?"

Mitzi shook her head "No, don't think she ever mentioned it."

"Was there anyone else?"

"I don't really remember, but I've only been here a few months. I had the impression Joy liked the nightlife though. Dancing and clubs and bars, you know that sort of thing."

"I do know." Ginny shivered. Robert had similar interests. And he preferred expensive restaurants.

None of it had been her scene though.

The bells over the door jingled as a group of women entered, and Mitzi waved at them.

"I gotta talk to those ladies. They want to plan a private women's luncheon here, and I can use all the business I can get."

Ginny offered her a smile. Under different circumstances, she and Mitzi might be friends.

"If you think of anything else, call me." Ginny pushed a business card into Mitzi's hand.

"Sure thing. Good luck with your story."

Ginny's phone dinged as Mitzi maneuvered around the corner of the bar to greet the women.

She pulled her cell from her pocket and checked the text. She had a message from the dating site Meet Your Mate. Rather, June Embers had a message.

A man named Karl Cross requested a date. She checked the man's profile in search of a photograph, but the one that was posted was taken from a distance and in shadows so she couldn't distinguish the man's face.

He looked to be about Robert's height. He was also dressed in a tailored suit, said he liked nice restaurants, fine wine and strong women.

All the things Robert had first said. All were true, too, except the part about the strong women. He wanted meek and docile. One he could control. Who'd do what he said, pleasure him and bow down to his every wish and order.

Her gut instinct told her that Karl Cross could be Robert. The only way to know was to meet him in person.

Nerves bunched in her stomach as she responded that she'd meet him at the bar called Whistler's Nightcap at seven.

GRIFF GRIMACED AS he walked to the sheriff's office. He hadn't handled the encounter with Ginny very well. But he didn't intend to allow another woman to use him—or fall for her lies.

Still, he felt bad for coming on so strong. She'd looked frightened, and he'd been raised better. His father would have given him a good talking to for his terse tone.

Why *had* he been so angry?

Because she's pretty and tempting and you want to trust her, but you don't.

Thunder rumbled, dark storm clouds gathering, rain on its way. He glanced back to where Ginny was parked. But she was gone.

Maybe she'd give up the story and leave town. Unless his instincts were right, and she was here for more than a story.

The wind battered the thin windowpanes as he entered Jacob's office. "I need to see Jacob," he told the receptionist.

"He's interrogating Wayne Norris at the moment."

"I'll wait in his office." Griff bypassed the deputy who was on the phone, then strode through the double doors and down the hall to his brother's office. Jacob's desk was a mess, but Griff noticed a grainy photo on the side of his computer. He leaned closer to see what it was, and realized it was a sonogram of Jacob and Cora's unborn baby.

A smile tugged at his lips. The Maverick family was growing. Odd that he hadn't pictured any of them married and now the longing for someone to fill his lonely nights with niggled at him.

Ginny's face teased at his mind.

Do not go there.

While he waited for Jacob, he seated himself and decided to dig deeper into Ginny. The fact that she was still here roused his curiosity even more.

He should have googled her before now but figured she'd be gone in a day and forgotten. But he plugged her name in and found two Virginia Bagwells. One was seventy-five and owned a pet store for cats in Maine. The other was deceased.

Next he entered the words *journalist* and *investigative reporter* and spent the next half hour researching various publications and articles but found no byline for a Virginia or Ginny Bagwell.

She said she was trying to break in to a TV network, so he researched those as well, but if she'd had any experience in the media, he couldn't find it.

Footsteps sounded behind him, and he glanced up and saw Jacob in the doorway.

"What are you doing?" Jacob asked.

Griff stood. "Ginny followed me from the morgue," he said. "I think she may know something about Joy's murder."

"Really?"

"Something's definitely off about her. She claims to be researching a story on arsonists and saw the news on TV, but she's been asking questions about Joy, how she died, if she was strangled."

Jacob's brows shot up. "She specifically asked about strangulation?"

Griff nodded. "Since you haven't released that detail, it made me wonder if the murder was what brought her to Whistler."

Jacob gestured toward the computer. "So, you were researching her?"

"I was, but so far she's a mystery. I can't find anything about a Ginny or Virginia Bagwell. It also struck me as odd that she came to me, and not you."

Jacob worked his mouth from side to side in thought. "Could be she's just a nosy journalist or that she's hiding something. Either way, it's worth looking into. I'll have Liam see what he can dig up." Jacob folded his arms. "Meanwhile maybe you should keep an eye on her."

Griff's stomach tightened. "I guess I could do that." He would just have to remain objective. "How'd it go with Wayne? Do you think he killed Joy?"

Jacob shook his head. "I don't like the bastard, but the creep has an alibi."

"He could have hired someone," Griff suggested.

"That's a possibility. My deputy is looking into his financials to see if he was in trouble or if he withdrew a significant amount of money lately, money he could have used for that purpose."

"How about insurance?"

"Joy's business was doing well. No major financial problems. Wayne was not a beneficiary on her insurance. She removed him from the policy when she filed for divorce. He also had no claims to the business."

"Maybe he was angry she cut him out."

"Could be," Jacob said. "But I have to start considering other persons of interest. I'm on my way to talk to Riley Thornton, the receptionist at the salon. Maybe she knows more about Joy's personal life."

"Tonight, I'll drop by the bar where Joy and I went," Griff offered. "Maybe the bartender saw her with someone else."

"Good idea. I'll meet you," Jacob offered.

Griff shook his head. "Let me go alone. Bartender might freeze up when he sees a uniform." Griff pointed to the ultrasound picture. "Besides, you have a family to go home to. How's Cora feeling?"

"Tired, but excited," Jacob said with a grin. "Nina's ecstatic about having a little brother or sister."

"I'm happy for you, brother." Griff suddenly felt antsy to leave. "Let me know what Liam uncovers about Ginny."

They agreed to stay in touch, and Griff left the office. Outside a few raindrops had started to fall, the clouds growing darker by the minute. He headed back to his truck, then decided to track down Ginny again.

Maybe she was back at the inn? He climbed in his truck, then drove past Mitzi's. Ginny's little sedan was there.

But she hurried out just as he neared the parking lot. He slowed and watched to see where she was going, his pulse hammering as he noticed her checking over her shoulder as she walked. She passed the mercantile and arts-and-crafts store, scanned the street as she walked. At one point, she ducked beneath an awning, then peered around the corner as if looking for someone.

Or…as if she thought someone was following her. What—or who—was she running from?

GINNY MADE HER way along the storefronts until she spotted the smoky ashes of Joy's Nail Salon, or what was left of it, which was a charred rubble of ash and burned materials. A cleanup crew had yet to clear the mess which seemed like a massive endeavor. Crime-scene tape flapping in the wind still cordoned off the area.

The businesses along the street nearest the salon included a barber shop, boutique, pet-grooming spa, novelty-and-gift store and a henna tattoo parlor.

Joy might have met a love interest from the barber shop. A frisson of nerves hit her as she entered the all-male establishment. The scent of aftershave and men's salon products wafted around her. Three chairs faced mirrors with barbers busy at work at their stations.

She offered the young man behind the desk a smile. He was probably early twenties, and sported a pony-tail and a diamond stud in his left ear. She introduced herself as a journalist and asked if he'd known Joy.

"Seen her around," the guy said with a scowl. "Too bad about that fire. She ran a nice place. We coordinated some marketing efforts. Some of our customers' wives liked to get their nails done while the men got a shave."

Ginny cleared her throat. "Was she seeing anyone in particular?"

The phone rang, and he shook his head. "Not that I know of." While he answered the call, Ginny stepped over and spoke to one of the other barbers, a fortyish man with a thick beard. His gaze skated over her, then he smiled. But his smile faded when she explained the reason for her visit.

"I don't know about her personal life," he said. "I asked her to dinner once, but she turned me down. Guess I wasn't her type."

"What was her type?"

He shrugged. "Like I said, I don't know anything about what she did on her own time."

She laid a business card on his workstation. "Please call me if you think of anything."

She received similar reactions from the other two barbers. None of them claimed to have dated Joy or knew who she might be involved with.

When she left the barber shop, she headed inside the pet spa. A curly-haired blonde about Joy's age was leading a white miniature poodle to its owner at the desk. Ginny watched as the groomer accepted payment and petted the dog goodbye.

The girl's name tag said Katie. Ginny introduced herself and asked about Joy.

"She did my nails," Katie said. "They get such a mess here when I'm working."

"Did you two discuss your personal lives?" Ginny asked, striving for subtlety.

Katie stacked fliers about an upcoming Pet Rescue event on the counter. "I told her about my boyfriend," Katie said. "She was a good listener."

"Was Joy seeing anyone?" Ginny asked.

Katie tapped her fingers on the desk. "Why are you asking? Do you think someone she dated killed her?"

"I don't know," Ginny said. "The police are investigating. But I'm considering a human-interest angle for my story."

Katie seemed to mull over that statement for a minute. "Well, I think there was a new guy she was seeing, but she didn't tell me his name. Bragged that he was really good-looking and charming and knew how to treat a lady."

"Did she have a picture of him or describe him?"

"Nothing specific, just that he liked to take her to nice places, expensive places, not like some of the losers she'd dated before."

"Where did they meet?"

Katie chuckled. "That was the funny thing. They met on a dating site. All my friends have been doing it, but all the men they connected with are creeps. A couple guys were into porn, one into guns and another into S & M."

"I've heard similar stories from other women," Ginny said. "Do you remember the name of the site she joined?"

Katie ran her fingers through her thick, sandy-blond hair. "I think it was called Meet Your Man. No, that's not right."

"You mean Meet Your Mate?"

Her eyes brightened. "Yeah, that's it."

Ginny's lungs strained for air. Tonight, she was supposed to meet a date from Meet Your Mate. Was Robert already looking for a replacement for Joy?

HE FLICKED THE lighter and watched the tip burst to life with a beautiful orange-and-red flame. He had been mesmerized by fire since he was a child.

Ever since the night he'd stood outside his own house and watched it burn to the ground with his mama in it.

The sound of the fire hissing transported him back in time.

HE WAS FIVE years old and his daddy dragged him outside and made him stand by the giant oak tree with the Spanish moss that dragged the ground like a witch's hair.

"Stay here!" Daddy shouted as he ran back inside.

But he didn't stay put. He sneaked up and watched his daddy and mama arguing in the kitchen.

"You'll never leave me," Daddy said. "Never."

"Give me the boy and let me go," Mama cried.

Daddy grabbed her arms and shook her. "You said till death do us part."

Mama tried to jerk free and run, but Daddy flung her backward against the wall. She stumbled and her head hit the counter. Then his daddy lunged at her and wrapped his hands around her throat.

He stood frozen. A scream of terror lodged in his throat as his daddy choked the life out of her. She flailed her arms and hands, struggling to yank free. But his daddy was too strong and mad, like one of the rabid dogs he'd seen running free on the deserted mountain roads.

The world blurred out of focus. Smoke filled the air. Or maybe it was the tears blinding him. He blinked and rubbed at his eyes, but they felt gritty.

When his vision cleared, Daddy shoved Mama to the floor. He held his breath to see if she got up, but she lay still, in a puddle on the black-and-white tile. Her red dress spilled around her like blood. Her eyes looked wide as she stared up at the ceiling. Her hands were curled by her sides. She didn't move.

Daddy lit the gas burner on the old gas stove, then tossed the match onto the flame. Then he turned and walked out of the kitchen.

A smile tilted Daddy's mouth and a calmness came over him like it always did after his father gave Mama one of the beatings. A loud boom sounded, then flames burst through the house. The windows exploded, spraying glass. Wood crackled and popped. The roof collapsed.

Daddy ran toward him. He snatched his hand in his and held it so tight it hurt. They stood silently, watching the flames eat up the old house and everything in it.

"That's what happens when your wife tries to leave you." Daddy said as he dragged him toward the old pickup truck. "She has to be punished."

He swallowed back a sob as his daddy pushed him into the truck. Daddy would punish him if he cried like a baby. "What about Mommy?" he finally whispered.

"Don't worry, son," Daddy said. "She should have listened like I told her."

Then his daddy started the engine and drove away without looking back.

He turned in the seat and watched the smoke float in the sky and the flames light the darkness.

He would miss Mama.

But the fire was so pretty he couldn't take his eyes off it.

Chapter Six

Griff felt like a stalker as he watched Ginny visit the barber shop and pet-grooming spa.

She was definitely investigating Joy's murder, not just a routine arson story. Could she have known Joy? If so, why not admit it?

His phone buzzed and he connected, hoping Jacob had more information.

"Where are you?" Jacob asked without preamble.

"I've been following Ginny," Griff said. "She came to Joy's Nail Salon, then went in and talked to people at the barber shop and pet-grooming spa."

"Stay close to her," Jacob said. "Liam said he couldn't find anything on her either. She must be using a fake name."

"The question is why," Griff muttered.

"Good question," Jacob said. "Meanwhile I talked to Riley. She's really torn up about Joy's death. Said a developer came in talking about buying up that entire row of businesses and wanted everyone to sell."

Griff's pulse jumped. "I take it Joy didn't want to sell?"

"No, apparently she was the only holdout. Owner of

the barber shop said he'd already found another spot if he sold. But Joy liked the location and didn't want to have to start over. Besides, the apartment space above was a perfect fit for her."

"Who is this developer?" Griff asked.

"Some guy from Asheville named Thad Rigden. Liam is running a background on him, and I'm going to have a talk with him when I locate him."

According to Ginny's business card, she was from Asheville. Was there a connection?

Jacob's words echoed in his head. *Stay close to her. She must be using a fake name.*

Griff decided to try a new tactic with her. He'd play nice. Just like his mother used to say: *you catch more flies with honey.*

Hell, he'd drip honey if necessary to find out why that pretty little woman had come to town and tried to use him.

GINNY HAD A bad feeling that Joy's match date might have led to her death. Then again, if Robert had dated her, he could have met her at a bar or even walked into the barber shop for a shave, seen her next door and made contact.

"Did Joy mention having problems with anyone?" Ginny asked. "Maybe an old boyfriend?"

"Her ex was definitely an issue." Katie waved to a customer with a sheltie as she entered the store. "Oh, and she and that developer butted heads."

"Developer?"

"Yeah, Thad Rigden. He's a big real estate developer who wanted to buy up all our stores and build condos here. Joy refused to sell when he offered her a deal. She liked the location and said Whistler didn't need fancy condos. They needed to support local small businesses."

"Were you going to sell?" Ginny asked.

Katie shrugged. "The money was good, and I needed it, so yeah. He promised to help me find another location. In fact, everyone was on board except Joy. Even her business partner was in favor."

"Joy had a business partner?"

"Yeah, a private investor," she said. "Although she never told me who it was."

Ginny's instincts reared their ugly head. The real estate agent would know the name of this investor. "So, I guess this investor stood to gain if the place sold. Or if an insurance settlement came from it."

Katie fidgeted. "You think someone killed Joy for money over her shop?"

"I don't know, just exploring theories," Ginny said.

Either way, she intended to talk to the developer. Her mind pieced together a scenario. Robert had been business savvy and could have posed as the real estate mogul.

"Do you have his contact information?" Ginny asked.

The woman with the sheltie was approaching with a cart full of items including a dog bed and chew toys. Katie reached inside the drawer behind the counter. "He left some business cards," she said and handed Ginny one of them.

"Thanks." Ginny laid her own card on the counter by the register. "Call me if you think of anything else."

She left Katie to deal with her customer, stepped outside then called the number for the developer. The phone rang three times, then the voice mail kicked on, so she left a message saying she was interested in speaking with him about some property for a business start-up, and that Katie had recommended him.

Maybe he'd know if Joy's silent partner was Robert, or he could give her another name.

GRIFF WANTED TO talk to Ginny, but his phone buzzed. His boss.

"Sorry, Griff, I know it's your day off, but we need help. Another wildfire, up at Pigeon Creek this time."

Dammit. He was only a mile from the firehouse, so he drove over and joined the backup team just as the first on-call squad peeled from the fire station. He geared up quickly, hoping for rain to help drown out the fire. Though the dark clouds were ominous and threatening, they hadn't yet unleashed. Still, the wind had shifted and picked up, adding to the problem.

His buddy, Trey, the lead today, radioed the GPS coordinates from the first squad and suggested Griff's team take the east area where they believed the fire had begun. Team one would hit the center. The wind was carrying it fast, catching dried leaves and trees and moving in the direction of the new cabins on the creek.

"We have a squad near the cabins, already wetting the area down to ward off the blaze from reaching the houses. If this builds up momentum, we'll need to attack it from above," Trey said.

"Copy that," Griff responded into the mike clipped to his uniform.

Flames lit the sky as the truck screeched to a stop; the sound of wood crackling and timber falling rumbled. This one had gotten out of control quickly.

He and his squad launched into action, rolling out hoses, raising ladders to be able to spray into the heart of the fire and hacking away vegetation inch by inch to keep it from catching in case the wind took an abrupt shift and the fire moved the opposite direction.

Heat suffused Griff, the odor of charred wood and debris rising in the air. Sweat beaded his skin inside his uniform, and the smoke was so thick he could barely see through his protective hat and face mask.

They worked for the next two hours, and finally got the damn blaze under control. Still they dumped more water on the embers to ensure the wind didn't stir it back to life. Griff prayed no one was caught in the forest or trapped inside the blaze. The smoke alone could kill a person.

As the area where the fire started slowly died, he began searching for signs of the point of origin and an accelerant. Heat scalded him through his clothing, preventing him from traveling too deeply across the charred ground. He moved to the edge and scanned the area nearest the creek.

The sight of several empty beer bottles caught his eye, along with footprints. He shone his light into the brush and spotted a pack of matches. The fact that they were the same brand as the ones he'd discovered at the previous fire suggested they were dealing with one arsonist. Or if this was a bunch of teenagers, the same group of kids.

He bagged the matches and bottles to send to forensics. A few feet away, he found an empty bottle of lighter fluid.

He'd known these fires weren't accidental, but now he had proof. Hopefully forensics could find a print somewhere on the items he'd collected, and they could stop this arsonist before someone was injured or a fatality occurred.

GINNY HAD QUESTIONED all of the business owners in the strip with Joy's Nail Salon. Each one confirmed Katie's story that they were on board to sell to the developer. The description of the developer could fit Robert, although none of them had seen him in person. And no one else had insight into a silent partner. Apparently, a female working with the developer had visited the property and made the initial assessment, then reported back to him.

Still gritty and achy from the earlier fall, she decided to return to the inn and shower before she met Karl Cross at the bar. She checked her surroundings and over her shoulder as she walked back to her car, then slid inside to drive back to the inn.

Once again, she had the uncanny sense she was being watched. She jerked her head around and scanned the parking lot. A man in a dark hoodie walked hurriedly toward a green Lexus. Another man in a suit and raincoat ducked into a sleek black Cadillac, although she couldn't see his face.

Was she paranoid?

For months after she'd left Robert, and after Tess's death, she'd thought she'd seen Robert everywhere. On the street, at the grocery store, in a car passing by, at the coffee shop… She'd told the police, but without proof he was following her, they couldn't do anything.

At one point, she'd thought she was losing her mind.

But she'd been certain he was watching her. That he stayed in the shadows taunting her. He'd left dead flowers on her car once. Another time he'd written a message in lipstick on her mailbox.

Every time an incident occurred, she moved. Hid out in dive hotels. Hostels. Shelters. Anywhere she thought she might be safe. She'd lived in her Asheville apartment longer than she'd lived anywhere in three years.

She had no home anymore. No family. No one who cared.

Swallowing against the lump in her throat, she surveyed the street and watched to see if the sedan followed her as she veered from the parking lot. Dark clouds rumbled, the sky overcast and dreary just like her mood.

She parked at the inn, tugging the hood of her raincoat over her head as she grabbed her computer bag. Gripping it in one hand, she kept the other one over her weapon in her coat pocket as she hurried up the cobblestone path to the front door. The owner of the inn had decorated the front door with a handmade wreath, and bird feeders dotted the garden area to the right. A path led through a flower garden that supposedly featured the innkeeper's love of roses, although nothing was blooming now.

Tess would have loved the garden. She would have painted all the beautiful colors with its lush green foliage and the backdrop of the mountains and sharp ridges rising above.

Ginny ducked inside the door, her heart aching as she climbed the stairs to her room. As she pulled her key from her purse and unlocked the door, an icy foreboding washed over her.

The cologne. She could smell Robert's cologne as if he was in the room.

Fear nearly immobilized her. If he had been here, was he inside? Had he picked the lock?

She held her breath as she poked her head into the room. The coverlet and pillows on the iron bed were just as she'd left them. Her suitcase lay open on the luggage rack. The welcome basket sat on the table, the ribbon still tied at the base.

It didn't appear anyone was inside.

Shoulders tense, she inched into the room. Had she left the bathroom door ajar?

She eased the hall door closed behind her, then pulled her gun at the ready and inched toward the bathroom. The door squeaked as she pushed it open and blood rushed to her head.

A message had been written in lipstick on the mirror just like the one Robert had written her before when he'd taunted her.

A message that said—*I'm watching, love. I'm always watching.*

GRIFF HAD JUST stepped from the shower when his phone buzzed. Jacob.

"Hey, man," Griff said as he connected the call.

"Did you receive my message about the forensics I sent to the lab?"

"Yeah, I told them to fast-track the lab work. I want to stop whoever's doing this *now*." Jacob paused. "I set up a time for us to talk to the students at a school assembly tomorrow. 10:00 a.m."

Griff rubbed the back of his neck where his skin still felt scalded from the heat. "I'll be there."

A tense second passed, then Jacob cleared his throat. "By the way, I questioned some of the shop owners by Joy's place. That reporter was all over town asking questions today just like you said."

Griff rubbed a hand over his eyes. "She's persistent at her job."

"Yeah, but she might just get herself killed nosing around. I'll pay her a visit and ask her to leave the investigation up to the law."

Griff dropped his wet towel to the floor and grabbed a pair of boxers. "Let me talk to her first," he offered. "She seemed spooked at the thought of talking to you."

"Probably because if she interferes, I can arrest her."

He hoped it didn't come to that. "I'll head over to the inn and talk to her now. Warn her that she needs to back off." Not that he expected her to listen. But it was worth a shot.

They agreed, and ended the call, then Griff finished dressing. He pulled on a button-down navy shirt with his jeans and combed his hair. He didn't know why he took the time with his appearance, but decided it was because he was headed to the bar to talk to the bartender after he left Ginny. Not because he wanted to impress her.

Five minutes later, he parked at the inn. A few rain-drops pinged the ground just as he reached the porch. Wind chimes tinkled as the breeze stirred them, and the scent of rain filled the air. He entered the inn, then went to the desk and asked for Ginny's room.

The owner's eyes flickered with interest as if she thought he was there on a date.

He silently groaned then climbed the stairs and knocked on the door to the Sunflower room.

Seconds passed with no response, and he knocked again. "Ginny, it's Griff. We need to talk."

Another second, then two. Finally, her voice. "Just a minute."

Footsteps sounded inside, then the lock turned, and Ginny appeared. The moment he saw her, he knew something was wrong.

Her face looked ashen, and a bandage on her fore-head made his eyebrows raise. It was mostly hidden by her hair but visible when she tilted her head sideways. Her hands also looked bruised, the palms scraped.

What in the hell had happened to her?

Chapter Seven

Robert's message kept replaying in Ginny's head. *I'm watching, love. I'm always watching.*

She hadn't been paranoid. Whether or not Robert had killed Joy, he was here in Whistler. And he'd been inside her room.

Nausea threatened, but she swallowed hard, determined to pull herself together. She inhaled sharply, rattled by Griff's appearance.

Why had he shown up right now?

She needed time to assimilate the fact that Robert was close by. That she'd thought she was prepared to confront him. To kill him. But now her courage was waffling.

"Ginny?" Griff's voice sounded thick with worry. He gently took her arm, closed the door behind him and guided her over to the bed. Her knees felt so pathetically weak that she sank onto the mattress. On some level, it registered that she hadn't been alone with a man since Robert. And that Griff was big and muscular and could probably overtake her if he wanted.

But the fear fogging her brain had nothing to do with Griff.

He knelt in front of her, gently lifted her hands and examined her palms. "Tell me what happened. You didn't have these at the café."

She looked at her palms in a daze. She barely felt the sting of the scrapes now, just the cold, hard terror of knowing Robert was two steps ahead of her. That she'd thought she might have control.

"What happened?" Griff asked again, his voice riddled with worry.

She looked into his eyes and saw genuine concern which nearly brought her to tears. But Robert had been a consummate liar, had pretended to care. Even after he hurt her, he'd kiss her and soothe her with tender looks and sweet nothings.

All lies.

She pulled her hands from Griff and straightened her spine. "I took a fall into the street earlier."

"A fall? It was an accident?"

"Of course," she said. "It was crowded, and I was crossing the street from the café after you left and wasn't paying attention and just tripped."

After hearing other abused victims' stories, she realized how lame her excuse sounded.

"That's why you're trembling now?" he asked. "That happened hours ago."

Ginny knotted her hands in her lap. She had to distract him from what had happened to her. "What are you doing here, Griff?"

Disappointment tinged his sigh. "I talked to Jacob. He said you were asking questions around town about Joy."

Ginny crossed her arms. "I did. And we've already discussed this. That's my job."

Griff cleared his throat. "Nosing around in a murder investigation is dangerous. You could get yourself killed." His gaze shot to her hands again, and Ginny lifted her chin.

"You're one to talk. You run into burning buildings and blazing forests for your job."

"I do it to save lives, not for some byline," Griff said, his voice taking on an edge.

Ginny's temper flared. "Maybe I'm doing it for the same reason. If I expose Joy's killer and he's a repeat offender, I might save another woman from the same fate."

Griff's eyes narrowed, and she wondered if she'd said too much. But he couldn't convince her not to finish this. Because this wasn't just a story or a byline she was after. She did want to save lives.

Including her own.

GRIFF STUDIED A fire methodically. Examined it for the point of origin. Analyzed the type of accelerant used to fuel the blaze. Utilized forensics to prove the arsonist's identity.

He needed to analyze Ginny in the same manner.

Obviously, logic was not working. And he'd bet his next paycheck that she hadn't fallen.

Warning her to back off had seemed like a wise idea. But she either was just stubborn, or...this case was personal to her for some reason. Had she known Joy?

Her statement about a possible repeat offender

echoed in his head and strained his patience. "What do you mean, if he's a repeat offender? Ginny, do you know who killed Joy?"

Her mouth tightened. "No, I was talking hypothetical."

Dammit, he didn't believe her. But he stepped away to wrangle his temper under control. He'd frightened her earlier at her car when he'd caught her following him, and something else had frightened her afterward.

More than anything he needed to win her trust.

"You do realize that by asking about this killer, you're drawing his attention to yourself and he might come after you?"

She winced slightly, her only reaction. "I do. But if I help catch him, it'll be worth it."

"Why is it worth risking your life?" he asked. "Did you know Joy?"

She shook her head although a sad look passed across her face.

"Because you think whoever strangled her killed before?"

She looked away this time and absentmindedly rubbed her finger over the scar on her wrist. A telltale sign he was right. And one that made him more curious about how she'd gotten that scar.

Concerned about her now, he lowered his voice. "Ginny, tell me what you know." He reached for her arm to trace the burn scar with his finger, but she jerked it away and crossed the room to the window. For a moment, she stood staring outside at the rain drizzling against the windowpane and the dreary sky.

She looked pale, sad and frightened. But beautiful,

like a lost child in a dark storm. The instinct to pull her in his arms pulsed through him, so strongly that he fisted his hands by his sides.

Pushing her would only make her run away.

GINNY ALMOST CAVED IN. Griff sounded so caring that for a moment, she forgot she couldn't trust him.

His brother was a man of the law. Griff saved lives.

They wouldn't approve of what she had planned for Robert.

But the idea of allowing him to comfort her teased at her resolve.

Even if Robert was here, he might not have anything to do with Joy's murder. There were other possibilities. She had to find the truth.

"Please, Ginny, I can't help you if you don't talk to me."

"I don't need your help."

"I think you do," he murmured.

Maybe she was out of her league. She needed to give him an olive branch, a half-truth, because he didn't appear to be backing off.

"All right," she said. "Sit down and we'll talk." She gestured toward the wing chair in the corner while she claimed the desk chair, needing distance between them. "But this is confidential."

His thick dark brow quirked up in response. "Go on."

She inhaled a deep breath, planning the story in her mind. If she kept practicing, she might become as adept as Robert at bending the truth. Although her stomach knotted at that idea. She didn't like deceiving others.

But she also detested the fact that the police had let Robert get away with murder.

"I was recently contacted by a victim who claimed a man she was dating tried to strangle her and then set her house on fire."

Griff squared his shoulders. "She survived?"

If only she had. "Barely. She went into hiding afterward, because she was afraid he'd find her again and finish what he'd started."

"Did she report the attack to the police?" Griff asked.

"She did, but it didn't go well." Ginny fought anger at the way she'd been treated when she'd first reported Robert's abuse. "He escaped."

"What was his name? Where is he?"

"She claims she met him on an online dating site, but when the police investigated, the photo had been taken down. Apparently, the man was savvy enough to delete his profile and wipe it from detection by the authorities."

"What about the FBI? Cyber experts?"

"They found nothing. He probably used a fake identity and profile before, and he's most likely created a whole new persona for himself now."

Silence stretched between them for a tension-filled minute. "What about a sketch?" Griff finally asked. "Did she work with a police artist?"

Ginny bit her lip. "I don't know. She didn't give me one."

"My brothers are different from this other cop,"

Griff insisted. "They aren't incompetent and will get the job done."

"Maybe. But first I have to know if the cases are even connected."

"She called you when she saw the news about Joy's murder?" Griff said, piecing her story together.

"Yes," Ginny said. At least that was partly true. "That's the reason I wanted to know if Joy was strangled, if the MOs were the same. If not, I can move on somewhere else to look for this man. But if it's the same one... Well, I want to nail him to the wall."

Griff remained silent for another heartbeat, then heaved a breath. "All right. I'll help, too. Ask her to send a sketch and I'll show it around town myself. And if you'll tell me the name the man used on his dating profile, I'll ask Liam to look into it."

Ginny shook her head. "I told you this is confidential, Griff. This woman trusted me, not the police. If I find out he's the one responsible, I'll keep you informed."

Griff stroked her arm gently. "Ginny, if you're right and this guy is a serial predator, he's dangerous and won't have any qualms about coming after you."

"I don't care," Ginny said. "I'm going to find him and make him pay for what he did to her."

GRIFF TRIED ONE more time to convince Ginny to talk to Jacob, but she refused.

"I shared this with you in confidence. She wants to remain anonymous," she said, her gaze daring him to argue. "I expect you to uphold that confidence."

He debated on whether or not he could.

He'd never been a liar or a user, and he didn't want to start now. Jacob had urged him to stick close to Ginny and see what he could learn, and he had. But now his interest was piqued in both what Ginny had relayed, and what she'd kept to herself.

That burn scar on her wrist meant she had been involved in a fire. She'd talked about an anonymous tip.

Had it been anonymous? Or someone she knew?

Or was it possible that she'd been a victim of the same man or some similar scenario?

Either way, the thought of her in danger disturbed him and roused his protective instincts.

He sat outside in his truck for a while, biding time until he went to the bar. But when Ginny hadn't ventured out of the inn a half hour later, he decided she'd play it smart and stay tucked in for the night.

He started his engine and drove to Whistler's Nightcap, hoping to glean more information about Joy's love life. The parking lot was filling up, a mixture of locals and tourists coming to the mountains for hiking and camping adventures. Soon the town would heat up with spring festivals and white-water rafting. Already hikers ready to explore the Appalachian Trail were piling in, gearing up at the local outfitters, sharing meals and drinks as they planned their excursions.

Most would never complete the two-thousand-mile trek from Georgia to Maine, but even a few hundred miles of the trail was an accomplishment that warranted a pat on the back and admiration from their families and friends.

Fletch would be busy rescuing half of them when they had accidents or suffered injuries or got lost, a common problem on the endless miles of forests and trails in the wilderness.

Griff secured his phone in his pocket, tugged his jacket hood up to ward off the drizzling rain and loped inside. But he couldn't shake the image of Ginny from his mind. She'd looked so vulnerable and small and proud. Dammit, that pride stirred his admiration, but made dread curl in his belly.

Loud country music pulsed through the crowded interior of the bar while a band rocked out on stage. The dim light helped conceal flaws for hopeless drunks on the prowl for a good-time girl for the night.

Once upon a time, he'd played that game. Joy had been part of it.

He'd learned his lesson and hadn't engaged since. Two women at the bar, midtwenties, attractive and built, wearing skimpy outfits, gave him flirtatious looks. He shot them a half smile then walked to the opposite end and slid onto a bar stool to face the door so he'd have a view of the dance floor where couples gyrated to the music.

The bartender, a bearded, broad-shouldered gym rat named Boone, flicked his hand up in recognition, and Griff ordered an IPA. He waited until Boone brought him the beer, then motioned that he wanted to talk.

"What's up?" Boone asked.

"You heard about Joy Norris being murdered?"

Boone nodded. "Yeah, sorry to hear it. Didn't the two of you date for a while?"

"Very briefly," Griff said. "But I learned she was married at the time and that was it."

"Most of the dudes here don't give a damn if a

woman has a ring." Boone made a low sound in his throat. "Truth is, half the women don't either."

A damn shame. His parents would still be married and faithful to each other if they were alive. He had a feeling Jacob and Cora, and Fletch and Jade would be the same. "Did you see Joy hanging out with anyone recently?"

Boone scratched his fingers through his beard. "She didn't come in that much. But she was here a couple of weeks ago with some guy in a suit. That's the reason it stuck out." He gestured toward the casual atmosphere. "He didn't seem to fit in."

"Were they getting along?"

"He was all over her," Boone said. "And seemed protective. Some other guy offered to buy her a drink, and the date turned all huffy and macho. I thought he was going to punch the poor bastard out."

Griff's suspicious nature surfaced. "What was the date's name?"

Boone scrunched his face in thought, then gestured to one of the waitresses that he'd work on her drink order. "Can't really remember. Something kind of uppity, like Winston or William."

"Can you describe him?"

Two guys leaned on the bar and called Boone's name. "You gonna get us a beer or talk all night?"

"Sorry, man, customers are waiting." Boone tossed the towel over his shoulder, picked up a mug and began to fill it from the tap.

"Just a quick description," Griff said.

"Tall, dressed well, sandy blond hair. Real intense guy. Not a body builder or anything but strong looking.

He had these beady eyes. Kind of dude you wouldn't want to mess with."

The waitress appeared for the beer, and Boone hurried to take care of the guys who were calling his name again.

Griff stewed over the information as he studied the crowd in case the man Boone described was in the room.

But someone else caught his eye. A woman with ivory skin and soft black hair who'd just come in the door.

Ginny.

Dammit to hell, what was she doing here?

Chapter Eight

Ginny had not been on a date since her experience with Robert. Not that this was a real date, but she had to pretend.

Nerves tightened her shoulder blades as she surveyed the interior of the bar. The country music and relaxed decor didn't fit with Robert. Typically, he preferred more upscale places although Whistler wasn't exactly big-city living so the choices were limited. And it was possible he was trying to keep a low profile to avoid detection.

She headed toward the right to the adjoining dining area where the music volume was lower as were the lights, creating a more intimate atmosphere. White tablecloths, each adorned with a vase of a single rose, added a hint of romance.

Her stomach churned. Robert would choose the more intimate side.

The hostess for the restaurant side was a tall blonde who wore a simple black dress with glittery jewelry. Robert's type. Although he had told her he had a thing for redheads.

She requested a table facing the door, and the hostess escorted her to a small table in a dimly lit section.

Clutching her purse, which held her .22, in her lap, she seated herself so she could see anyone who entered or left.

Karl Cross said he'd be wearing a navy sport coat and khakis, a little underdressed for Robert, but it might be his attempt to fit into the town and not draw suspicion to himself.

She ordered water and a glass of white wine although she left the wine untouched. Didn't want alcohol interfering with her reflexes if she needed to defend herself. She sipped her water and waited, surprised at the number of single women crowding into the bar area.

She had never been a fan of the bar scene, had always thought it dangerous. The online dating site had been just as bad. The attractive profiles could easily sway a woman into believing she'd met her Prince Charming, yet in reality the person behind the face on-screen might be an amphibian beneath the facade.

A man with silver-tipped dark hair entered, then a cowboy in a Stetson. The cowboy headed toward the bar while the other man paused and looked around, then turned to the dining area. He was wearing a dark sport coat. She tensed as he scanned the room.

Not Robert. Was he Karl Cross?

She took another sip of water as he started to cross the room, but he bypassed her table and joined a middle-aged woman at the table near her. She was so busy watching the couple kiss that she didn't notice another man approaching until she felt his presence beside her table. A shadow moved into her vision, and she looked up, her chest clenching.

He was tall, dark haired, medium build, nice looking. But he wasn't Robert.

He offered her a cocky smile. "June?"

"That's me," she said, itching to leave already. Although if Robert hadn't killed Joy, she could have met another predator online. This could be him.

He slid into the chair and raked his gaze over her. Her first instinct was to jut her chin up in challenge, but she was supposed to be quiet, shy, bookish June so refrained.

"A pleasure to meet you," he said. "You have an interesting profile."

She gave him a shy smile. "So do you. Do you live in Whistler?"

He shook his head. "I have a cabin in the mountains nearby, so I come here for relaxation between business trips."

"Do you travel a lot?"

The waitress appeared and he ordered a whiskey. "Just in the States, wherever the deals are to be made," he said as the waitress left.

"What kinds of deals?"

"Oh, a little of this and that."

Her distrust rose. He was being evasive. "Where's your home base?" Ginny asked.

"Charlotte. What about you?" he asked.

"I'm here visiting family, my grandmother," she said ad-libbing. Better he think she had someone who would miss her if she disappeared unexpectedly.

They made small talk for another few minutes, then she decided to broach the real reason she'd met him. "You don't look like you'd have trouble meeting women," she said. "Do you engage in a lot of online dating?"

He chuckled. "I *don't* have trouble," he said. "But I'm looking for a specific type."

Her skin prickled. "And what type is that?"

A flicker of interest sparked in his eyes. "Someone quiet. Humble. Women these days are flashy and forward. They don't appreciate a man taking care of them."

She barely resisted slugging him. He sounded like Robert. "Have you dated anyone else from Whistler?"

His smile disappeared. "What does that matter?"

"Just wondering if there's an old flame around who'd get jealous if she saw us together?"

"No one at the moment." His eyes darkened. "It pains me to say the last woman I was seeing died suddenly."

Ginny bit her lip to stifle a reaction. "Oh, my goodness. You weren't seeing that pretty woman named Joy, were you? I arrived in town the day after she died in that horrible fire."

The ice in his drink clinked as he lifted it for a sip. "Did you know her?"

She shook her head. "No, I just saw the news. I heard she liked to play around."

His hands tightened into fists on the table. "That's what I'm talking about. Women who aren't faithful. I can't tolerate that."

If the woman he'd dated was Joy, he'd just confirmed a motive for murder.

He reached for her hand and stroked her fingers. "But you wouldn't be like that, would you, June? You wouldn't lie to a man?"

She had had enough. He wasn't Robert, but he was despicable anyway. She pushed away from the table and stood. "You know, Karl, I don't think this is going to work."

He tightened his fingers around her wrist so hard she winced. "What? Aren't you going to give me a chance?"

She gritted her teeth. "I just don't feel like we're right for each other." She yanked at her hand to pull free, but his grip grew more intense.

"That's not fair, June. Sit back down—"

"Let the woman go."

Ginny gritted her teeth as she looked up and found Griff staring down at her and Karl with a lethal expression on his chiseled face.

Nothing riled Griff more than a bully manhandling a woman. And this creep looked as if he'd gone from friendly to psycho possessive in seconds.

The man released Ginny's wrist then angled his head and shot Griff a venomous look. "Who the hell are you?"

Griff fisted his hands by his sides. Resorting to physical force wasn't his style, but if it meant protecting Ginny and he was provoked, he wouldn't back down either. This jerk was decent-size, but he could take him in a skinny minute.

"A friend of the lady's," Griff said coldly.

Ginny shot him an irritated look and absentmindedly rubbed at her wrist, which was red from the man's tight grip.

"I can handle this, Griff," she said stiffly.

He arched a brow in challenge. Did she know this jerk? Was she actually going to defend him?

Karl shoved his chair back. "What is this? Some kind of hustle?" He narrowed his eyes at Ginny. "You plan a date, then your boyfriend jumps in for fun?"

Shock flashed across Ginny's face at the implication. "No. But this date is over."

She snatched her purse, threw it over her shoulder and brushed past Karl and Griff.

Karl stood as if to go after her, but Griff blocked his path. "You heard her. It's over. Touch her again and you'll answer to me, someone more your size."

Karl squared his shoulders, anger radiating from him. "Don't worry. She's not my type anyway."

Griff barely resisted the urge to punch the jerk. Instead, he stepped back and went after Ginny himself. The music blared louder from the bar area, and a line dance had kicked up, boots pounding the scarred wooden floor.

He hurried out the door and searched the parking lot. Ginny was climbing in her car, so he jogged over and caught the door just before she could close it. Her eyes widened, a sliver of fear darkening the depths that made him feel like a heel. He threw his hands up to indicate he meant no harm.

"Are you okay?" he asked gruffly.

Her breathing rasped out. "Yes. And by the way, I had the situation under control." Stubborn pride laced her voice.

"Of course, you did," he said. "But when I see a man roughhousing a woman, I can't help but step in. My father taught me to respect women."

His comment seemed to soften the defensive expression on her face. "Then thank you. But I really was fine."

He leaned closer to her in the open doorway of the car. "What was that about anyway? I thought you were just visiting town. Did you know that man?"

She cut her eyes away, avoiding him, then flexed her fingers around the steering wheel as if debating on how to respond. Finally, she sighed and looked back at him. "I don't want to talk about it here. Meet me back at the inn."

She bit her bottom lip, then started the engine. But she scanned the parking lot as she pulled away. Was she afraid the man inside would follow her?

Or was she was running from someone else?

GINNY DROVE TO the inn, relieved to see that Karl Cross didn't follow her. As stern as she might have been, Griff was much more intimidating.

Although why had he come to her rescue? She didn't think he liked her or wanted to talk to her. Had he followed her to the bar?

She parked and climbed out, her nerves on edge. Had Robert snuck back inside the room?

Griff parked behind her and walked over to her car. "Let's meet in the parlor," Ginny said. "There's wine and coffee at the buffet in the evenings."

Griff walked beside her as they made their way up the path to the porch. The earlier rain was dissipating, yet the wind had picked up again, blowing leaves across the lawn and sending the wind chimes on the porch into motion. The tinkling reminded her of the holidays when she and Tess had been children and had enjoyed their mother's endless litany of jingle bells that she strung everywhere. Her mother bought them silly Christmas socks every year to wear for their annual Christmas pajama photo by the tree. When she was six and Tess was four, they'd separated to choose each other's presents and ended up buying each other the same book of paper dolls.

Tears burned the backs of her eyelids. Each memory of her sister refueled her rage and anger.

Griff opened the door, and they entered the lobby, then made their way to the parlor. Thankfully it was deserted so they had the room to themselves.

She poured a glass of wine for herself, then offered Griff one from the buffet. He shook his head and chose coffee, then joined her in the seating area. The wine helped soothe her jangled nerves as she warmed herself by the fire.

Griff seated himself across from her in the big club chair. "Come on, Ginny. Who was that man?"

"I had a date," she admitted.

He raised a brow. "You came for a story and now you're dating? I don't understand."

He didn't have to, but he obviously wasn't going to let it go. Her plan to use him hadn't worked at all. He was too damn smart.

"I told you that I received a tip from an abuse victim," Ginny said. "She met the man online through one of those dating sites."

Griff's jaw tightened. "Let me guess. You joined that site hoping to meet that creep?"

Ginny ran her finger along the rim of her glass.

"Like I said earlier, he disappeared. She's terrified he's looking for her."

Griff cleared his throat. "Did you get a description of the man?"

Ginny shifted. "Medium build, sandy-blondish hair, dressed well. He likes nice restaurants and wine."

Griff tensed. "The bartender gave a similar description of a man Joy was in there with once. He thought his name was Winston or William."

Ginny paused with her glass halfway to her lips. "He said his name was Karl Cross. He became defensive when I asked about Joy, and he said the last woman he dated died suddenly."

"I'll ask Jacob and Liam to investigate him."

Ginny traced a finger around the rim of her glass. "I told you I don't want to talk to the cops. Whatever I share with you is confidential."

Griff made a low sound of frustration in his throat. "For God's sake, Ginny, I'm just trying to help. You have to get over this paranoia about the police."

"That's impossible when this woman's attacker bought off a cop to find out where she was hiding, and he nearly killed her."

Tension charged the air between them. "I'm sorry that happened, but I assure you my brothers are decent. They'll do everything they can to track down this bastard and make him pay."

Ginny leaned forward, desperate to believe him.

But his brothers would only get in her way.

GRIFF STUDIED GINNY for a moment. Although he sensed she'd told him multiple lies, if what she'd said about the cop accepting a bribe was true, he understood her distrust of the law. Arguing with her would only push her further away. He'd learn more by keeping her close and agreeing to work with her. "All right, I'll keep your confidence," he replied. "But trust works both ways. You aren't allowed to print anything I tell you unless I clear it with Jacob first."

Ginny pasted on her game face. "Of course."

"Do you think the man you met tonight was the same one who attacked your source?"

She shook her head. "I don't know. But have your brother check him out. If he dated Joy, he might be the man you're hunting."

"What online dating site did you use?"

Ginny stretched out her legs. "Meet Your Mate."

Seeing that man put his hands on Ginny bothered Griff more than he wanted to admit. He told himself his reaction was simple protective instincts that he'd feel for any woman, but something about the pained note in Ginny's voice tore at his heartstrings on a more personal level.

"You're playing with fire by trying to lure this predator," he said huskily.

Ginny finished her wine and stood. "You're not going to change my mind. So, remember our deal."

He clenched his jaw as she walked away, removed his phone from his belt and punched Liam's number to ask him to dig up everything he could on Karl Cross and that dating site. He'd also ask him to look at other cases involving strangulation and arson.

Like it or not, he didn't intend to let Ginny use herself as bait and get herself killed.

Chapter Nine

Ginny watched Griff leave with a mixture of admiration and trepidation. He was a strong man. Could be dangerous. She'd seen that flare of temper in his eyes when he'd ordered Karl to release his grip on her. And he'd pinned her with a stare that made her feel uncomfortable.

Yet as much as she hesitated to trust him, she didn't think he'd hurt her. At least not physically. His protective streak seemed to be *for* her, not in a possessive way, but in the chivalrous way she'd only seen in the movies.

Could it be real?

It didn't matter. She was here for one reason and one reason only. To find the man who'd killed her sister. As soon as she reached her room, she'd call that real estate developer again. Maybe if she was persistent enough, he'd return her call.

Moving on autopilot, she scanned the main lobby of the inn as she approached the stairs. Not that she thought Karl Cross would have followed her here, but a woman could never be too careful. One lunatic in her life was enough.

Another reason to avoid men.

She'd just made a deal with one though. *To share information, nothing more.*

She mulled over the tidbit Griff had shared. The man Joy was with at the bar could have been Robert. If he'd gone by William or Winston, maybe she could find his profile on the dating site.

A light rain began to fall again, and fog formed on the picture windows in the front. For a moment, her vision blurred, and she thought she saw a man standing by the trees flanking the drive.

He wore a long dark trench coat and hat and seemed to be staring at her.

Robert?

Heart pounding, she slid her hand over her purse, then reached inside for her weapon. The wind kicked up, trees swaying outside. A tree branch snapped at the windowpane. Rain fell, fat drops splattering the glass.

She hurried to the front door but when she opened it, there was no one there.

Heaving a breath, she shut the door, turned and fled toward the stairs. Her foot slid on the slick wood, and she grabbed the rail to steady herself, then forced herself to slow down as she climbed to the second floor. If Robert was out there, he was gone. At least for the moment.

She glanced down the hall at the top of the stairs to make sure he hadn't somehow gotten inside, then hurried toward her room. Hands trembling, she fumbled with her key, then jammed it in the lock and opened the door. The cloying scent of Robert's aftershave still clung to the air. Or was it fresh?

Entering on shaky legs, she pulled her gun and scanned the sitting area then rounded the alcove to the bed. A cry lodged in her throat at the sight of the white lilies lying on the bed.

Lilies are for purity, Robert had said. *Just like I want you to be pure for me.*

Tears spilled over as she surveyed the room and eased toward the bathroom. A bath had been run. Rose petals floated in the water. A bottle of champagne sat on the bathroom counter with two champagne flutes waiting.

And then the note.

Sleep tight, love. Soon you'll be in my arms again. Very soon.

GRIFF PHONED JACOB to relay his conversation with Ginny as soon as he made it to his cabin.

"Did she mention where this attack happened? In North Carolina or another state?" Jacob asked.

Dammit, he should have probed her for more information, but his specialty was to extinguish and investigate fires, not serve as a detective in a homicide investigation. "No. The next time I see her I can find out. But since she's from Asheville, it's probable that it occurred in North Carolina."

"I'll ask Liam to look for a case that fits this scenario."

Griff entered his house and punched in the code to the alarm. "Anything on the forensics from the last fire?"

"The lab just called. They have a match on some prints. A couple of teenagers at the high school. A kid named Jerome Miller who was caught shoplifting cigarettes at a gas station, and Randy Henner. Randy was caught driving without a license."

"Both are petty crimes, and a big jump to escalate to arson," Griff said.

"I know. If these teens are already taking risks and looking for a rush, booze might have triggered their behavior to escalate."

"Boys will be boys getting out of hand," Griff muttered.

"Maybe. The assembly at the school is tomorrow at ten. I contacted the principal and told her I plan to question the boys afterward."

"I'll be there."

"One more thing, Griff. Bring a picture of Ginny if you can get one, and Liam can run it so we can find out who she really is."

An uneasy feeling tightened Griff's chest. He didn't like spying on anyone behind their back. But Ginny was playing a dangerous game, and he didn't want her to get hurt, so he agreed.

Maybe Liam would confirm she was exactly who she claimed to be, and that he could trust her.

He told Jacob about the dating site. "If Joy met her killer on this site, we need to explore it."

"I'll call forensics again and see if they've been able to recover anything from Joy's computer." Jacob paused. "See you tomorrow."

Griff muttered agreement, then poured himself a whiskey. He needed some sleep, but how could he sleep when he was worried a killer might be targeting Ginny?

GINNY STOOD FROZEN and trembling, reliving every horrific memory of Robert in her head as the rose petals bobbed gently across the bathwater.

When they'd first met, Robert had turned her head with flattering compliments and sweet nothings he'd whispered in her ear. He'd wined and dined her and promised to support her while she finished her degree. He'd carried her shopping bags at designer boutiques and lavished her with expensive jewelry to ensure she dressed in style.

She'd insisted she didn't need fancy clothes or jewelry, that she was a simple girl who liked homemade meals and quiet nights, one who dreamed of a family of her own someday.

He'd given those words lip service, but three months into the relationship, he announced he didn't want children, and he certainly didn't want her body to be disfigured with a pregnancy. Appearances mattered to him. She had to work out. Diet. Learn how to dress and behave.

Be the perfect wife.

That meant looking good on his arm and entertaining his friends and clients in the home he intended to design for them. A glass house where she would have to tiptoe around on eggshells for the rest of her life.

She'd realized then that they weren't a match. Home was about family and loving each other, not being perfect or about surface appearances or impressing rich strangers who tossed money around like it was nothing.

That night she'd told him so, and he'd become irate.

Told her she owed him and should be grateful for all he'd done for her.

That he would never let her go.

She lifted her fingers and traced them across her throat, a suffocating feeling overcoming her as she recalled his fingers pressing into her vocal cords. His words had hammered home her reservations and she'd decided she had to leave. When he'd found her packing, he'd announced she had to be taught a lesson then he'd tried to strangle her.

She'd screamed and fought him, but he'd dug his fingers into her windpipe and for a moment she'd almost passed out. But in the struggle, she'd managed to grab a lamp and she'd smashed it against his head. He released her and she'd run for the door, but he'd chased her down, then given her a beating she'd never forget.

A lesson she deserved, he claimed as she lay bleeding and hurting on the floor. Later, he'd pulled her against him, comforted her, then run her a bath and sat beside her to nurse her wounds as she'd shivered in shock.

But his plan had backfired. The rage had built inside her that night like a fire that couldn't be extinguished. Instead of coercing her as he'd planned, he'd done the opposite. The first strike across her face had cemented her determination to leave him and given birth to hatred.

Outside the wind banged against the glass, startling her back to the present. She swallowed hard to chase the memories back into the darkness, then summoned her strength. Tess's sweet face flashed behind her eyes, and she wiped at tears.

She hurried to the bedroom door and locked it, then dragged the dresser in front of the doorway. Furious at Robert for unnerving her with his games, she let the bathwater run down the drain, threw the rose petals into the trash and poured the champagne down the sink. The bottle went into the trash, then she snagged the lilies from the bed and added them to the pile.

Fueled with adrenaline, she opened her laptop and began combing the dating site for a man named William or Winston who fit Robert's general description. Twenty minutes later, after scrolling through a dozen Williams, and three Winstons, she found a possible match. William Roberts.

Roberts? Could he have used his first name as his last in the profile?

Again, the man's face was hidden in shadows. He had a short beard, neatly trimmed, and stood by a Mercedes wearing a dark pin-striped suit. Enjoyed French wines. International cuisine. Had made his money in the stock market.

His profile fit.

She sent him a message saying she'd like to meet, then pulled on her pajamas, grabbed her gun and crawled into bed. She kept the bathroom light on and turned on her side, so she faced the door with her weapon gripped in her hand, ready to shoot if he decided to slip in during the night.

THE NEXT MORNING Griff showed up at the school assembly a half hour early to meet Jacob.

"No word from Liam yet," Jacob said. "But he's

investigating Ginny Bagwell, murders and attempted murders involving strangulation and arson."

Griff had thought about Ginny all night. Something wasn't right with her story. If Jacob uncovered information he could share with her, maybe she'd open up.

Both the principal and the school counselor, Linette Akron, met them in the gymnasium as the kids filed in. Griff was not a fan of public speaking, but this was a serious matter. He'd spent the morning compiling photos of the recent fires and had thrown a few less graphic shots of burn victims into the mix. His audience was young and impressionable, but God knows they'd become somewhat desensitized to violence and trauma from the news and school shootings and had to face the reality of the dangers of the fires. The counselor stood by in the event a student needed help or became emotional.

The principal called the assembly to order and explained the reason for the meeting, then introduced Griff. Jacob situated himself by the door nearest where the two boys in question had been strategically seated.

"We're here today because of a very serious matter," the principal began. "In the past few weeks, there have been a series of wildfires along the AT in our area, one of which was not far from the school and the town of Whistler." She gestured to Griff. "Today one of our local firefighters from station house 7 is here to discuss these fires."

Griff stepped up to the podium and cleared his throat, then opened with a general explanation of arson. The PowerPoint he'd prepared showed pictures of the actual fires and how close they'd spread to campsites and a residential area. When the photographs of burn victims and corpses appeared, shocked gasps reverberated through the gym.

"We're discussing this today because we need your help." Griff clicked to show a photo of the beer bottles and matchbook recovered from the scene. "These items were discovered near the point of origin of the fire." Another photo revealed the lighter fluid. "Although it's possible the fires were small campfires where someone was drinking and partying, then the fire got out of hand or wasn't extinguished properly, evidence suggests the fires were intentionally set."

The teens in the room began to shift and make noises of discomfort.

One of the boys in question looked panicked and glanced at the exit sign, but Jacob moved to the edge of the row where he sat, made eye contact with him and shook his head.

"We need you to let us know if you've seen or heard anything, any chatter, about these fires at school, off the school grounds or online." The students shifted again, fear and panic flitting through the group.

Griff adopted a nonconfrontational stance. "I'm sure none of you want to see anyone hurt or killed by these wildfires. If you have information, please tell your parents, the counselor, or call the sheriff. Because if there are injuries or casualties, the arson charge will be elevated to manslaughter or possibly homicide."

More gasps, indicating he'd gotten their attention.

The counselor stepped up to offer her services, emphasizing anonymity. She'd already established a special drop box for the students to report instances of bullying, drugs or weapons on campus, and urged the students to use it now.

As soon as the principal dismissed the assembly and the kids began to file out, Jacob cornered the two boys in question. Due to the fact that they were minors, their parents had been asked to meet in the counselor's office where the boys would be questioned.

Jacob assured Griff he'd keep him abreast if he got a confession, and Griff paced the entryway in the school.

All night he'd been haunted by images of Ginny being attacked or strangled.

He hoped to hell she was safe.

HE THUMBED THROUGH the photographs he'd snapped of Reese while she darted around Whistler asking questions about Joy Norris's murder. She'd thought she was hiding out all this time, and he'd let her believe it.

Decided time and distance might make her miss him. Appreciate him.

Laughter rippled in his throat as he traced a finger over her heart-shaped face. Joy had reminded him so much of Reese with her auburn hair that when he'd closed his eyes and pounded himself inside her, he'd imagined it was Reese.

But then she opened her sassy mouth to talk in that nasal like voice, and he saw her face. Makeup smeared and too-red lipstick. She'd looked ugly.

Just like the others. No one could replace Reese because she was perfect.

And she was his.

Once he got her back, he'd make sure she knew it. And she'd never leave him again.

Chapter Ten

Robert was toying with her. Playing hide-and-seek to frighten her. Enjoying keeping her on edge.

And it was working.

Ginny kept her gun in the bathroom while she showered and dressed. As she checked the dating site on her computer, her phone pinged that she had a message, and she quickly checked it. It was Thad Rigden, the real estate developer buying up the block of businesses housing Joy's Nail Salon.

The voice sounded slightly higher-pitched than Robert's, but if this man was Robert, he could have disguised it. He suggested they meet for coffee at Mitzi's at ten-thirty, so she agreed, then spent the next half hour scrolling through online dating profiles reviewing every William and Winston she could find.

The man she'd pinged the night before responded that he'd like to meet her for a drink around five. She confirmed, then stowed her gun inside her purse, grabbed her jacket and headed outside. She checked the hallway in all directions, then hurried downstairs. Pausing at the bottom of the stairwell, she scanned the entryway and parlor. An older couple was enjoying coffee and a late breakfast, and two young women dressed for hiking rushed out the door, backpacks slung over their shoulders.

A gusty breeze whipped her hair around her face as she stepped outside, and a cigarette glowed near a tree at the edge of the woods.

Robert?

He hadn't smoked cigarettes when she'd known him but had occasionally enjoyed a cigar. She thought about the wildfires Griff had been putting out and wondered if Robert could possibly be responsible. Deciding she needed the exercise, she veered onto the sidewalk leading to the heart of town, keeping one hand securely on her purse to give her easy access to her gun if needed as she walked to Mitzi's.

A midmorning crowd filled the café, a mixture of retirees, campers and hikers preparing to set out on the AT. She waved to Mitzi as she entered, then started to take a booth near the front, but Mitzi motioned for her to follow her.

"That real estate developer is back here," Mitzi said as she led Ginny through the center of the café to a booth in the corner near the back.

Ginny's stomach tightened as they approached. The man was facing the rear wall with his face away from her. He had short, neatly groomed brown hair, and a gold signet ring glittered from his hand as he lifted his coffee cup for a sip.

Robert had worn a gold signet ring with the letter *R* etched in the design. The imprint of it on her cheek had lingered for days after he'd hit her.

GRIFF WAITED FOR Jacob in the entrance of the school while Jacob questioned the two boys he'd identified as persons of interest. Memories of attending Whistler High flooded back.

Griff had played defense on the high school soccer team and helped them make it to the state championships. School shootings and drugs and violence had not been part of his experience. Boys had roughhoused, enjoyed off-roading and met girls behind the bleachers to make out. Not one for online social media, he'd attended high school pep rallies, football games, dances in the gym and he'd hung out by the river with friends.

On camping trips, his father had taught him and his brothers how to read maps, fish and kayak. He'd loved the fresh air, outdoors and endless miles of forests. Sure, he and his brothers had sneaked a few beers in their day, but they'd been harmless and respected the land and the people in town.

His father had run for sheriff to protect the residents and had instilled the same values in him and his brothers. Each of them had become first responders to honor him.

Then that fire had taken his life. Gone in a minute.

Griff should have insisted his father stay outside that horrible day. His father hadn't been prepared to run into the fiery building. Hadn't been wearing safety equipment. No oxygen mask or helmet or fireproof clothing.

But the fire had created such chaos, and with so many lives in danger, his father hadn't thought once about joining the rescue attempts. Dozens of sick patients, disabled, people in wheelchairs and bedridden needed help. Mothers and children and babies were among the needy, too.

They'd tried to save them all. And even then, they'd failed.

Footsteps dragged him from the haunting memory. Jacob approached him, grim faced. Griff expected him to escort the boys to the jail, but he was alone. The teens' parents were accompanying the boys through the exit.

Jacob paused to shake hands with the principal and counselor, then joined Griff.

"What happened? Aren't you making arrests?" Griff asked.

Jacob motioned for them to go outside, and they left together, then walked over to Jacob's squad car.

Jacob scrubbed a hand over his chin. "Both boys admitted to drinking in the woods, to smoking a couple of cigarettes and building a campfire on two occasions. But they claim they covered the fire with mounds of dirt before they left."

"Could have accidentally started back up."

Jacob shook his head. "That's just it. Both kids have alibis for the nights of the wildfires that spread. Parents confirmed they were home studying for tests during the time of the first fire, and one of the teachers verified that the boys play baseball and had an away game during the time of that last one."

Griff muttered a frustrated sound. "If they didn't set the fires, maybe some other kids are responsible."

"That's possible, but I'm beginning to wonder if it was teens."

"Why do you say that?"

"The boys mentioned seeing a man in a long coat

and hat with binoculars on a hill near the locations of the fires. They both insisted they'd seen his footprints around before, up around Raven's Ridge."

"I'll go back and search that area," Griff said. "If whoever they saw is our arsonist, he may have left some evidence behind."

GINNY SLID HER hand inside her purse and gripped her gun as she walked around the table. Her legs felt shaky, but anger heated her blood as she braced herself to face Robert once more.

The man stood and lifted his hand, the signet ring glittering beneath the overhead light. This man was the right height and build, but his eyes were set farther apart, his nose slightly longer, and his forehead not as high. Not Robert.

Relief mingled with frustration. Dammit, she wanted to get this over with. Make Robert confront her so she could...kill him? Could she really pull the trigger?

Tess's sweet face taunted her, and she swallowed hard. Yes, hell, yes, she could.

But this man hadn't killed her sister. She was wasting her time. Unless...he'd killed Joy and the similarities were coincidental.

The man extended his hand. "Thad Rigden. You're Ginny Bagwell, the woman who called about looking for property in town?"

Ginny nodded and claimed the chair across from him. Mitzi appeared, and she ordered plain coffee while he ordered a latte.

"Tell me about yourself, Ginny," Thad said. "Where are you from and what do you do?"

"I live in Asheville," she said simply. "And actually, I'm a journalist."

His eyebrow rose. "I thought you were looking for property for a business." He sipped his coffee. "Or did I misunderstand your message?"

"I'm sorry to mislead you," she said, deciding to opt for a half-truth. "I talked to Joy Norris's neighbors and they said you offered to purchase her property. That you had plans to rebuild the entire block."

His friendly smile faded. "That's true. Everyone except Joy agreed to sell. But I thought I could convince her to do so in time."

"Really?"

"Yes, I suspected she was holding out for more money, so I was working on securing a more lucrative deal for her."

"I see. But now that she's dead, it'll probably be easier to take over."

He narrowed his eyes. "Actually, that's not how it works. If she didn't have a specific will dictating who the property went to, it will go into probate. That could take months which will slow down the entire project."

That was true. "Did she have a will?"

Irritation carved frown lines around his mouth. "I don't know. Since the police ruled her death a homicide, nothing can happen until the investigation is complete."

"One of the other store owners mentioned that Joy had a silent partner. Do you know who that was?"

"No. If I had, I would have tried to convince him or her to talk some sense into Joy." He studied her with hooded eyes. "Now, Ms. Bagwell, why are you asking me these questions?"

Ginny knotted her hands in her lap under the table. "I had the impression the two of you were more than business acquaintances."

A flicker of unease settled across his features. "We had dinner a few times, but it was mostly business. I thought if I showed her my plans for the development, she'd be swayed into selling."

"But it didn't work?"

"No, she was stubborn," he muttered.

"That must have angered you, especially if your business plans relied on her cooperation."

A muscle ticked in his jaw. "If you're suggesting that I killed Joy because she refused to sell, you're way off base. Maybe you should talk to the sheriff instead of running around making accusations."

"I did speak to him, but he isn't sharing."

"That's for damn sure. I asked him what happened, but he shut me down. Even implied that I might have killed her to get hold of her property, just like you did." He released an angry sigh, stood and tossed his napkin on the table. "If I were you, Ms. Bagwell, I'd go back to Asheville. If you keep running around making accusations, you might end up like Joy."

GRIFF CALLED FLETCH, explained his conversation with Jacob and asked him to meet him at the put-in to the trail near Raven's Ridge. There, Griff led the way. Three miles in, they passed the point of origin for the latest wildfire.

The ridge overlooked the burned area, so the arsonist could have set it, then climbed to higher ground and watched it sizzle along the forest floor, eating up leaves, twigs and brittle grass as it spread.

Although crime-scene investigators had combed the area, he and Griff searched the territory again to make sure they hadn't missed something. When they were satisfied they hadn't, they climbed upward toward the ridge, following the path leading to the top. More rain threatened as dark clouds rumbled and swallowed the light from the sky.

Griff and Fletch hiked past trees so thick they had to turn sideways to weave between them. When they reached the top, the steep overhang jutted out over the woods below and offered an expansive view of where the fire had started.

The perfect place for an arsonist to watch his handiwork and bask in the glory as the flames licked higher and higher.

Griff and Fletch divided up and searched separate areas, the threat of bad weather forcing them not to waste time. Near a cluster of hemlocks leading away from the overhang, Griff spotted boot prints that had been somewhat protected from being washed away by the rain the night before. He shone his light along the edges and thought they might be able to make a cast, then noticed a path of crushed weeds a few feet from the prints.

He panned his light across the brush. Something shiny was trapped in the weeds. He pulled on gloves, and stooped to his knees. His fingers brushed over the shiny metal object, and he freed it, then held it up to examine it. A lighter—fancy, expensive, with the emblem of a black panther on the side.

Not one teens would own.

A hiker on the trail could have dropped it. But considering the location where he'd found it and the proximity to the latest wildfire, it raised suspicion. He bagged it and put it in his pocket, then strode over to Fletch where he finished making the cast of the boot print. They searched for another hour. Unfortunately, they found nothing else. Rain threatening, they hiked down the mountain to their vehicles.

"I'll run these by Jacob's office," Fletch offered.

"Thanks." The lighter might belong to the arsonist, but the fact that Joy's business and home had also burned down was seeming less like a coincidence. And more like they could be connected.

Which led him back to Ginny Bagwell.

She'd been shaken the night before. Had bruises where she'd fallen—or been pushed. He'd warned her she was flirting with danger.

What if something had happened to her while he'd been gone today?

GINNY SPENT THE afternoon at the coffee shop researching Thad Rigden on her computer. She looked for anything she could find indicating he was shady, dangerous or that he might have killed Joy out of anger over the fact that she refused to sell.

He had been through a nasty divorce settlement, which had gone public when his wife sued him for half of their assets, assets that amounted to almost a million dollars. The wife had filed a restraining order against Thad during the divorce proceedings with claims of intimidation tactics.

Had he used those tactics on Joy and the situation

had spiraled out of control? Was he so desperate for the investment opportunity to replenish the money he'd given his wife that he'd resort to murder?

The clock on the wall ticked off the minutes to the next hour, and she realized it was time to meet her next date from Meet Your Mate. She hurried back to the inn and changed into a nice sweater and black slacks, then walked to the wine bar William Roberts had suggested.

As always, she checked her surroundings and seated herself to face the doorway. For the next hour, she watched couples and individuals come and go, but her date didn't show. Wondering if she'd misread the time and place, she checked her phone for messages and reviewed the original interchange. No. She had the date, time and place correct.

The creep had stood her up.

Annoyed, she polished off the one glass of merlot she'd allowed herself to sip while waiting, paid the bill, gathered her purse and headed outside. More dark storm clouds threatened, thunder rumbling, and she increased her pace hoping to make it back to the inn before another deluge of rain descended.

The sun had come and gone while she was in the wine bar, and night had fallen with the temperature dropping again, adding a crispness to the air. Just as she passed the alley between Mitzi's and the craft store, footsteps pounded behind her.

She halted, sliding her hand to open her purse, then spun around to see who was there. A shadow moved into her vision, then suddenly jumped her. She tried to steady herself, but two strong hands shoved her backward and she hit the brick wall and fell into the dark alley.

Chapter Eleven

A shadow in the alley just past Mitzi's caught Griff's eyes as he drove toward the inn. He slowed, wondering if it was a lost tourist or someone attempting to break in the back door of the café. Occasionally drifters or vagrants Dumpster dived for food outside the restaurants. With tourist season beginning, sometimes seedy or questionable loners crept in to hide out on the trail, so it could mean trouble.

He eased into a parking spot at the diner, climbed out and walked toward the alley. Sounds of scuffling and voices echoed from the dark corner.

"Get off me, you bastard!"

Griff's instincts roared to life, and he darted into the alley. Ginny. She was on the ground fighting off an attacker. Before he could reach her, she shoved the man off her. Then she raised her feet and kicked him hard. He flew backward with a grunt, then dove at her again. But she lurched to her feet and threw her arms up in a defensive move that looked as if she'd been trained in self-defense. The man went for her throat with both hands, but she balled her right hand into a knot and punched him in the face. He bellowed, blood spurting from his nose, and lunged at her.

Enraged, Griff glanced in the alley in search of a stick or something he could use as a weapon, but it was too damn dark to see. Clenching his hands into fists, he jogged toward the creep. The man must have heard him, because he turned his head toward Griff. Shadows clouded Griff's vision, and the dark hoodie the man wore hid his features. The only thing he could tell was that he was medium build and height and wore all dark clothing.

His sound of rage rent the air, then he darted down the alley in the opposite direction.

Griff ran toward Ginny, calling her name. She seemed startled to see him and was trying to push herself up to stand. Her hair was tangled, her clothes disheveled, her eyes wide with fear and anger.

He gripped her arms to steady her and surveyed her features for injuries. Blood dotted her lower lip, and her cheek looked red. The damn bastard had hit her. "Are you okay?"

She nodded, but she was trembling and swayed as if dizzy. He pulled her up against him and wrapped his arms around her. "It's okay. You're safe now." He rubbed slow circles over her back and dropped a tender kiss in her hair. "It's over. He's gone now and can't hurt you."

She gripped his arms, her breathing erratic and choppy. Griff soothed her again, then helped her to the bench in front of Mitzi's. "Stay here and call Jacob. I'm going after him!" He didn't give her time to protest. He squeezed her arm again, then took off running down the alley.

He jogged to the end, then checked both directions. A flash of something across the street caught his eye, and he raced across the intersection. By the time he made it to the other side, he'd lost sight of the figure. Halting by the streetlight, he scanned the parking lot and storefronts, but he'd disappeared.

Dammit.

Heaving a breath, he studied the area again, but the only people he saw were a couple walking their dog and an older man pushing his walker toward a Cadillac near the Italian restaurant. Frustrated but concerned for Ginny, he hurried back down the alley and found her still waiting on the park bench in front of Mitzi's. She looked shaken and angry as he approached her.

He dropped onto the bench beside her. "Did you call Jacob?"

She shook her head.

"Why not?"

She rubbed at the scar on her wrist. "I told you I don't like the police."

Griff had had enough of her stubbornness. "Ginny, you were just attacked. That man could have killed you."

When she lifted her head, the emotions in her eyes nearly brought him to his knees. "I know that. But I was prepared."

His mind raced. "You may have taken a few self-defense classes, but he still could have overtaken you. For God's sake, you've been asking questions about Joy's death. That could have been her killer."

"I'm well aware of that."

Griff pulled his phone from the clip on his belt. "We have to report this to Jacob. And this time I refuse to accept no for an answer."

She reached up and placed her hands over his. "Please, Griff, don't."

"I'm sorry," he murmured. "Jacob has to know."

The disappointment in her expression made guilt knot his belly. But he pressed his brother's number anyway. Like it or not, he didn't intend to stand by and watch men attack women in his town and get away with it.

GINNY'S FIRST INSTINCT was to run. She could flee town, drive to another place and start hiding out all over again.

But that was no life. And doing so gave Robert the power he wanted over her.

He'd said she'd never escape him. And even in hiding, she hadn't because he dominated her thoughts. She looked for him on every corner, in every store, in every restaurant or café she went to. He haunted her sleep at night and every waking minute of the day. His menacing voice whispered her name when she stepped outside, or even in the shower. Especially when she was alone at night.

She'd been alone now for three years. Ever since he'd taken Tess from her.

She straightened her spine. This time she would not run. She would stay and fight. For Tess. And for herself.

"Let's go to my truck," Griff said. "We can wait on Jacob there."

She nodded although she couldn't quite look at Griff. He might see through her if she did.

Now that the adrenaline of the attack was wearing off, pain racked her body. She rolled her shoulder to alleviate the soreness and flexed her hands. Suddenly cold through and through, she began to tremble.

Griff walked her to his truck and unlocked it, then helped her inside and started the engine. He retrieved a blanket from the backseat. "Come here." He leaned toward her and gently wrapped it around her. Tears burned the backs of her eyelids.

Tears she refused to let fall in front of him.

But his tenderness touched a chord deep inside her, and she allowed him to pull her up against him and hold her for a minute.

"Are you hurt?" he murmured against her hair.

Just her pride. But she bit back the words and shook her head no.

"Did you see his face?" he asked.

Had she? She closed her eyes and struggled to re-call the details of the assault. She'd been so careful, watching everywhere she went. But he'd come out of nowhere and jumped her from behind. He was strong. About Robert's height and weight.

Had she smelled his cologne?

"Ginny, did you recognize him?"

"No," she said honestly. She had her suspicions but, she couldn't be certain it had been Robert. Robert would have said something more. He wanted her to know he was watching. He would have whispered her name to taunt her, or at least used his pet name for her.

Love.

His tone had been so endearing in the beginning that the nickname had made her heart swell with affection. She'd felt lucky that he'd chosen her.

God…

She'd thought he'd take care of her, be her partner for life. But the day she'd realized the true man beneath the facade, his tone had changed drastically.

If he was watching her and he saw her talk to the sheriff, he'd assume she'd told the police about him. That would only intensify his rage.

"Do you want to talk about the attack?" Griff asked gruffly.

She lifted her head and blinked away emotions she didn't want to feel. No man could be as tender and tough as Griff appeared to be. It wasn't real.

She couldn't allow herself to believe that it was.

GRIFF RUBBED GINNY'S BACK in slow, soothing circles. She felt so small and vulnerable in his arms that he wanted to keep her there where she was safe.

He hadn't liked seeing that man jump her. Hadn't liked it one damn bit.

She might think she was tough, but that man outweighed her by at least fifty pounds.

Jacob drove up beside Griff's truck, lights twirling, and Griff reluctantly pulled away. He couldn't become involved with Ginny when she was keeping secrets.

He opened the door, stepped out and met Jacob by his truck.

Jacob folded his arms and glanced at Ginny. "What happened?"

"I was driving over to check on her when I saw her in the alley. Some guy attacked her, and she was fighting him off."

Jacob raised a brow. "Did you get a look at him?"

Griff shook his head. "Not a good one. Medium height and build dressed in all dark clothing. Wore a hoodie that half covered his face."

"Does Ginny know who it was?"

"She claims she doesn't and that she didn't see his face."

"You believe her?"

A tense second passed. Then Griff cleared his throat. "I want to."

Jacob muttered a curse. "All right. Stay with her and I'll search the alley, then we'll go to the station to file an incident report. I'm going to ask a couple of my deputies to search around town as well."

Jacob retrieved his flashlight and crime kit from his car and headed down the alley. Griff got back in his truck. Ginny had recovered slightly, brushed through her hair with her fingers and looked a little calmer. Although she sported a bruise on her cheek now, and her knuckle was scraped. Anger at the sight churned in his belly, and he gritted his teeth. "Jacob wants to search the alley, then we'll head to the station to file an incident report."

"That's really not necessary," Ginny said. "The man is long gone, and I can't identify him."

"Maybe he left some evidence behind in the scuffle," Griff said. "Something that will help us nail the creep."

Ginny fidgeted and turned to look out the window. Silence stretched between them as they waited.

"What made you decide to go into investigative journalism?" he asked.

She pursed her lips in thought. "My father was a journalist," Ginny said. "He used to travel the world and uncover stories about cover-ups with large corporations. I thought it was interesting that he helped people by exposing the truth."

Griff had never thought about journalism like that.

She shifted and twisted her hands together. "When I was little, I carried a notebook around and eavesdropped on people's conversations. Then I'd make up elaborate stories about what they were talking about or where they were going." The memory brought a smile to her face.

"Your father must be proud of you," he said quietly.

"He died when I was twelve. A hit man for one of the companies he was investigating," Ginny said, pain lacing her voice.

Griff understood about wanting to please and impress your father. "I'm sorry you lost him that young. Did the man who killed him go to prison?"

"Yes, but it took a couple of years for the police to make the case." Ginny swallowed. "You lost yours in the fire that happened in Whistler, didn't you?"

"You did your homework."

"I'm sorry." Her tone grew soft, sincere. "He died a hero though."

"Yeah, but my brothers and I want justice for his death. And we won't give up until we get it."

THEY HAD MORE in common than Ginny thought.

His comment made her question herself though. Would her father be proud of her?

No. She'd been a fool to fall for a slick charmer and should have recognized the signs that he was abusive before she agreed to the second date.

But she'd worn blinders and been snowed by his compliments, his gifts and attention. Tess had always been the pretty sister, the one the boys chased, while she'd buried her nose in a book and been more interested in researching stories on the internet than relating to students her own age.

And now Tess, his pretty little princess, had died because of Ginny's stupidity and foolishness.

Her father had also stood for good, had wanted to expose the seedy side of big corporations and help the underdogs who were unknowing victims.

What would he think about her plan to avenge Tess's death?

"Jacob is back," Griff said, cutting into her thoughts.

Ginny steeled herself against her emotions. Griff was a stubborn man. No sense arguing with him at the moment. He started the engine and followed Jacob to the police station. Ginny's nerves bristled as she entered, the memory of begging the police for their help hitting her with the force of a fist. The skeptical looks. The questions. The pitying stares.

The fact that she'd trusted them and one officer had betrayed her just as Robert had.

Who could she trust now?

Jacob led them past the receptionist and down a hall to his office. A deputy glanced up as they passed, a curious look in his eyes, unnerving Ginny even more.

Jacob gave her a visual once-over, his expression grim. "First of all, do you need a doctor?"

She shook her head. "I was just shaken, that's all."

"Your cheek is bruised, and your hands scraped," Griff cut in.

Ginny glared at him. She didn't need him pointing out that she'd nearly lost the battle with the man.

Jacob gestured for them to sit, and he returned a couple of minutes later with two coffees. He gave one to Griff and offered the other to her. Chilled from the ordeal, she took the cup and cradled it in her hands just to warm herself.

"This is a waste of time," Ginny said before Jacob could speak. "I didn't see the man's face. I can't give you a description, and I don't know who he was or why he jumped me."

"You're nosing around into a murder investigation," Jacob said. "That sounds like reason to me."

The two men exchanged silent looks that Ginny didn't quite know how to read. A brotherhood bond, she guessed. Just like she and Tess had once shared as sisters.

"Walk me through your day." Jacob slid a legal pad in front of her. "Write down the names of anyone you talked to." His voice was blunt. "And don't leave out anyone. Including the men you met on that dating site."

Ginny barely stifled a gasp. "How did you know about that?"

Jacob shrugged. "Griff mentioned that's how your anonymous source met the man who hurt her, so that would be a logical place to start."

She let his comment slide. If Robert hadn't killed Joy, one of the men from the site or the real estate developer could have. Jacob could investigate them and free her up to deal with Robert.

Unless William Roberts had been Robert. He could have set up the date to lure her away from Griff, then watched from afar as she waited on him to arrive. Then he'd stood her up, followed her and attacked her in the alley.

She quickly jotted down the names, then pushed the pad toward Jacob.

He folded his arms and studied her. "Do you have a sketch or photo of the man this source of yours dated? The one who allegedly attacked her?"

Ginny stood, furious. "I'm working on it." She turned and glared at Griff. "This is the reason I said no police. I don't like being interrogated as if I'm a suspect."

"Miss Bagwell, I'm trying to find out who assaulted you *and* solve a murder investigation," the sheriff said. "Without your cooperation, that's impossible."

She tapped the notepad. "There's your list."

She started for the door, but Griff cleared his throat. "Ginny, wait. Is there anyone else who would want to hurt you?"

His plan was working. Reese, who called herself Ginny now, was on edge. By now, she must have seen the flowers he'd left for her in her room. And she'd gotten his message. Knew he was watching.

That he'd have her soon.

Rage knifed through him though as he remembered that big fireman rescuing her in the alley. Hell, he'd been on the verge of coming to her rescue when the bastard jumped in to be her hero.

Had she started hooking up with him? With other strangers?

Apparently so. She'd rejoined that damned dating site. He'd been monitoring it for months just in case she resurfaced.

Worse, the fireman seemed to be buddy-buddy with the sheriff. Mitzi said they were brothers.

Had Reese, Ginny, told the police about him? Had she shown them a photo from his first profile?

It didn't matter. He didn't look like that anymore. Even she wouldn't recognize him on the street.

Although she would remember when he got her alone. She'd remember everything.

Chapter Twelve

Griff's question echoed in Ginny's ears. *Is there anyone else who would want to hurt you?*

She hesitated, then pointed to the list. "I gave you the names of everyone I've talked to since I arrived. You can talk to them and then tell me if one of them attacked me." Head held high, she left the office and walked through the hallway to the front door.

Outside, the sky was dark, wind whipping through the trees and making the traffic light sway in the intersection. Rain still threatened, the temperature in the low fifties, although the wind chill made it feel more like thirty in the mountains.

She stepped outside, scanning the street, the hair on the nape of her neck bristling. Even though she'd left Robert, she felt as if he'd been with her, smothering her, his claws sunk deep into her psyche, every day since.

It had to stop.

She'd just reached the corner by the traffic light to cross the street when she heard Griff call her name. She tensed, bracing herself for a confrontation.

"You're not walking back to the inn alone," he said huskily.

The concern in his voice touched her. "Griff, I appreciate you coming to my rescue earlier, but I'm fine now. I just want to go to my room and rest."

"All right. But I'm going to make sure you arrive safely."

"That's not necessary."

"Yes, it is. You were attacked once tonight. What if that guy comes back for you?"

"He probably just wanted my wallet and is long gone," Ginny said as she quickened her pace.

"You don't believe that and neither do I," Griff said. "If he targeted you because you're asking questions about Joy's murder, he must want to stop you."

Ginny ignored the twinge of guilt she felt for fudging the truth with Griff. He seemed sincere, like he was really worried about her safety. Realizing there was nothing she could say to deter him from accompanying her, she lapsed into silence until they reached the inn.

She glanced up at the quaint two-story house, desperate to remember that beauty still existed amidst the ugliness that had become her life. But her breath caught at the sight of a shadow in her window. Her hand automatically moved over her purse, and she itched to reach inside and draw her weapon.

"Thanks for walking me back." She turned and headed up the porch steps, but Griff stayed on her heels.

"I'll walk you to your room," he said quietly.

The intensity in his eyes made her stomach flutter. "Griff, just go. I don't need a babysitter."

"More like a bodyguard," he said, his voice thick.

She had needed one three years ago. Had asked the police for one. But they hadn't had the manpower.

It was too late now to start over. And definitely too late to start anything with this sexy fireman.

If Robert was waiting for her in her room, she wanted to see him and get it over with so she could leave town before Griff had to find out the truth about why she'd come to Whistler.

GRIFF GENTLY TOUCHED Ginny's arm. Jacob had caught him as Ginny rushed out the door. Liam had found another case where a woman was strangled, and her house set on fire afterward to cover her death.

A woman named Tess Taggart from Raleigh.

He wondered if Ginny knew about the case. She'd claimed her source had survived, but if she'd done her research and found out about this other woman, that might have triggered her to make a connection to Joy.

"Come on," he murmured. "I want to take a look at those bruises. You might need medical attention."

"I don't," she said.

He chuckled. "Humor me. EMT training is part of my job."

"For goodness' sakes, you're a pest," she said, a note of irritation to her voice.

He chuckled. She was a feisty, independent little thing. "Aww, Ginny. A gentleman makes sure a lady gets home safe and sound, all the way to her door."

Ginny clamped her teeth over her bottom lip. "I haven't been with any gentlemen lately."

He raised a brow. Her comment raised more questions in his mind. "Well, my mama and daddy taught me to be one."

They'd reached the porch, and he opened the front door. Ginny fidgeted. "Thank you, Griff, but I'm inside now. I'll be fine."

"To your doorway," he insisted.

Anger flared in her eyes, and she sighed then walked past the parlor to the staircase. He followed, scanning the entry and room in case her attacker had slipped in and was posing as a guest. If the creep who'd assaulted her had done so because of Joy's murder, he'd probably been watching her and knew where she was staying.

Griff had also noticed her reaction when she'd looked up at the window as if disturbed by something. Was someone in Ginny's room?

More curious than ever, he cupped her elbow with his hand and guided her up the staircase. "I'll just make sure you're tucked safely inside, then I'll leave for the night."

She shot him an annoyed look, then reached for her key. Her hand trembled and for a moment, she simply stood there as if afraid to go in. Or was she afraid he would?

Was she afraid of *him*?

His stomach clenched at the thought. Maybe he had come on too strong. But he was only trying to protect her.

And find out what she was hiding. If she knew who'd killed Joy, she needed to talk.

She fiddled with the keys and dropped them, so he picked them up and unlocked the door. Through the open doorway he spotted the bathroom door that had been left ajar and the bed where a red lace nightgown lay. Had she left out a gown to wear for a lover? Could that be the shadow he'd seen in the window?

Maybe she had a boyfriend back home who'd decided to join her in Whistler?

The scene in front of him certainly looked as if it had been staged for a romantic rendezvous.

A sea of rose petals trailed the floor from the doorway to the bed, then dotted the coverlet. Champagne sat chilling in an ice bucket with two flutes beside it. A box of expensive chocolates was on the pillow.

He narrowed his eyes. Not just a box of chocolates. A box with a photograph lying next to it.

A picture of a young woman who resembled Ginny.

The color drained from Ginny's face, and she staggered sideways and gripped the edge of the doorway with a groan.

Griff grabbed her arm to steady her and caught her as her legs buckled beneath her.

What in the hell was going on? If this was a romantic rendezvous, she didn't look happy about it.

THE PHOTOGRAPH… TESS… Her precious little sister.

Emotions clogged Ginny's throat, and the world blurred into a fog of memories. The last few times she'd seen Tess. Christmas. Three years ago. They'd made eggnog and sugar cookies and gorged on them as they watched their favorite holiday movie.

Then the spring festival in Boone where Tess had

rented a booth to showcase her paintings. She'd been so excited that day to sell three of her original pieces to people who'd been enthusiastic enough about her style to mention her to local art galleries.

With their parents gone, it was just the two of them, and they'd pinky sworn to celebrate every holiday and birthday together.

After their father's death when their mother realized how fragile life could be, she'd made Ginny promise to take care of Tess if something happened to her.

But she'd failed her mother. Her father. Her sister.

Tess could have enjoyed a long, exciting and successful career as an artist. She'd dreamed of traveling to Paris one day and painting along the Seine River.

But all her dreams had been cut short. Her life snuffed out with senseless violence.

All because Ginny had allowed herself to fall for a slick psycho like Robert.

She should have been the one who'd died.

"Ginny, what's going on?"

Griff's hand at the small of her back was gentle but firm. So was his voice.

"Were you expecting somebody tonight?"

Was she? Yes. She'd known he was here.

She had to pull herself together.

Releasing a weary sigh, she stepped inside the room. Her fingers itched to pull the gun, but her gut instinct screamed that Robert was already gone. He was playing out his fantasy game of tormenting her.

"Ginny, please talk to me," Griff said in such a quiet, soothing tone that she gestured for him to come in and to close the door.

Angry at Robert for his sick need for control and at herself for allowing him to still rattle her, she stiffened her spine.

"Were you expecting someone? A boyfriend maybe?" Griff asked.

She dropped her purse on the table by the door, then strode to the bathroom and peeked inside. Another bubble bath waiting. More rose petals. The scented soap he'd chosen for her. The one she thought was so sickening sweet it was nauseating.

Griff was right behind her and looked over her shoulder. "Am I interrupting something?"

For the first time since she'd met Griff, relief that he'd insisted on following her flooded her. Yes, he was interrupting. But apparently it wasn't time for her to confront Robert face-to-face. The demented jerk was making a statement, indicating he would choose the time.

Just like he wanted to be in control of everything else.

A fit of anger overcame her, and she dipped her hand into the tub to release the water, then wiped her hand on the towel and hurried back to the bed. She snatched the picture of her sister and pressed it to her chest, then raked the rose petals onto the floor with one hand, crushing them beneath her boots.

Griff stepped back, hands raised, confusion marring his face. Then understanding, as if he realized for some reason she needed to vent.

She didn't need to simply vent. She needed Robert out of her life forever.

Exhausted from the fight with her attacker and emotionally drained from Robert's intimidation tactics, she sank into the chair in the corner. Griff stood by the door, shifting onto the balls of his feet, his steady breathing the only sound in the room.

She sat in silence, clutching Tess's picture in her hands as she tried to gather her composure. The clock in the room ticked away the minutes. Thunder rumbled softly outside. The creak of footsteps in the hallway echoed through the doorway.

Griff knelt in front of her. "I know it's been a helluva day. You were attacked. And now it's obvious someone was in your room. What's going on, Ginny?"

She shook her head, too tried to pretend any longer.

"Do you know who was here?"

She released a shaky sigh then looked into Griff's eyes. The kindness she saw reflected in the depths tore at her resolve to keep her secret. Damn Robert for putting her in this position. For changing her...

"Do you?" Griff asked in a low tone.

She nodded numbly.

"Who was it?"

She squeezed her eyes to stem tears, then shook her head. She didn't want to share her story with Griff. It was too humiliating.

He lifted her wrist and rubbed slow circles across her palm, then traced the burn scar on her wrist. "Does whoever it was have something to do with this?"

She gave a small nod.

He rubbed his thumb across her chin and lifted it, so their gazes locked. Robert's had been filled with seduction and lies.

Griff's were more serious, somber, filled with a quiet, tender understanding and kindness that she'd never seen before in a man. He was strong. Tough. Dealt with life-and-death situations. Saved lives. He cared about others.

He could hurt her if he wanted. Not physically because he wasn't that kind of man. A rarity.

But emotionally. Because she liked him. Was starting to trust him.

Shame filled her. Would he help her if he knew the truth? Or would he look at her the way she saw herself—as the woman who got her little sister murdered?

GRIFF DIDN'T LIKE the pieces of the puzzle shifting and connecting in his head. Pieces of hidden truths he suspected had brought Ginny to Whistler that were personal.

She wasn't just chasing a story. At least not just *any* story.

He gently took the picture from her and studied it. The girl in the picture looked younger than Ginny. Hair a soft blond, hazel eyes, a slight pug nose. Similar, but different. A relative?

"Who is this?" he asked softly.

She ran her finger over the woman's face. "My sister. Her name was Tess."

Griff tamped down a reaction as the truth dawned. Tess Taggart, the woman from Raleigh who was murdered. "What happened to her?" he asked, desperate for her to explain.

"She's gone." She stood, wrapped her arms around her waist and walked over to the window. Rain began to patter the panes and fog blurred the view to the outside, cocooning them into the warmth of the room.

Although Ginny was shivering.

"What happened?"

"I don't want to talk about it."

Maybe not, but he sensed she needed to. He tried to recall everything she'd told him, deciphering through it for the truth in her story. "The man who set all this up? Did he kill her?"

She closed her eyes, her lower lip quivering. "He did."

"Was she dating him?"

She shook her head. "No. He didn't even know her."

Griff twisted his mouth in thought. He hated guessing. She'd told him about an anonymous source, had said the woman escaped. Had she lied? Was there really a source?

Liam's report echoed in his head. "How did she die, Ginny?"

Her eyes remained closed as if she was reliving the painful memories. Or maybe concocting another lie to tell him.

"She was strangled, wasn't she?" The truth made his stomach knot. "Like Joy? That's the reason you came to Whistler isn't it?"

She didn't have to answer. The gut-wrenching agony on her face told him everything.

He couldn't help himself. She looked so vulnerable and broken that he crossed the room and pulled her into his arms. "You believe the same man who killed your sister killed Joy. And he was in your room. He knows you're here looking for him?"

She nodded and leaned into him, her chest heaving up and down with emotions. "Yes. And it's my fault they're dead," she murmured. "All my fault."

Chapter Thirteen

Ginny's chest eased slightly as she finally confided in Griff. Shame followed.

She'd carried the burden of guilt alone for so long that it was more than humbling to admit it out loud. Griff would look at her differently now just as she looked at herself differently. The contempt she felt for her actions was overwhelming.

But at least now he knew, he'd be repulsed and leave her alone.

He slowly released her and looked into her eyes, his jaw clenched. "What do you mean? It's your fault?"

She folded her arms across her chest, bracing herself for his disgust. "Tess didn't know the man who killed her. She wasn't dating him. I was."

Griff arched a brow. "You're the anonymous source, aren't you?"

She nodded. She might as well confess everything now. "I met him on a dating site. All my friends were doing it and said it was safe, as long as we met in public."

His jaw tightened. "Go on."

"He was nice and charming at first, showered me

with compliments and gifts, wined and dined me, bought me expensive jewelry and designer clothes."

"And then?"

"Then he became possessive." She drummed her fingers over her arms. "He alienated me from Tess, from friends. All he cared about was how I looked on his arm and that I become the *doting wife*." Her skin crawled at the memories of his voice as he tightened his fingers around her wrists and crawled on top of her.

"One day I'd had enough and told him I was leaving, but he…didn't take it well."

Griff's lips curled into a frown. "He hit you?"

Shame reddened her cheeks. "He beat the hell out of me. But with the first blow, I knew I had to get away from him."

"God, Ginny." He reached for her, but she threw up her hands. She didn't want to be touched right now. Didn't want his pitying look. "Did you go to the police?" he asked.

She shifted from foot to foot. "I followed the rules and filed a protective order. But that only incensed him. He began stalking me. Following me everywhere I went. Showing up at the coffee shop and at school where I was enrolled in journalism classes. He left little gifts to remind me he was watching me. He was always watching." A shudder coursed through her. "When his gifts and notes and romantic gestures didn't work, he followed me to my apartment one night and broke in. That night I wound up in the ER. He told the doctors I fell down the staircase."

A muscle ticked in Griff's jaw. "Did the police arrest him?"

"Yes. He spent a few hours in lockup, but he had money and friends with deep pockets. By nightfall, he was back at my place and enraged that I had the gall to have him put in handcuffs. He said I'd pay."

And she had.

With her sister's life.

Griff folded his hands together. "Then what happened?"

"I asked the police for protective custody, but they didn't have the manpower. I moved, created a new identity and thought I'd escaped, but he bribed a cop and found me again."

So that part of the story was true. "No wonder you don't trust the police," Griff said.

"That time, he tied me up and left me for days, so I'd learn my lesson." Her heart hammered. "Finally, I managed to untie myself and crawled out the window. I drove to Tess's to stay with her until I could figure out what to do. On my way though, he called and said he warned me I'd be sorry." Her breath caught in her chest at the sound of his sinister voice leaving that message on the phone. "When I got to Tess's house, it was on fire. I ran in to save her, but it was too late." Tears choked her voice as the image of Tess's pale, lifeless face surfaced.

"So, you see now. My sister would still be alive if I hadn't been such a fool and gone out with him."

GRIFF HAD SENSED Ginny was lying, that there was a story behind that scar on her wrist, but he hadn't considered she was an abuse victim or that a maniac had murdered her sister. No wonder she'd taken self-defense classes.

"Did the police investigate your sister's murder?" Griff asked.

"They did, but they didn't find his prints in the place or evidence proving it was him. Then he disappeared."

"And you think he came here, that he connected with Joy and murdered her?"

"It fits," she said in a pained whisper.

Griff gestured toward the flower petals she'd raked on the floor. "He did all this, too."

"He's cruel, likes to taunt me. He wants me to know that I can't escape him, and that he'll punish me again."

Griff raked a hand through his hair, his anger boiling.

"He has to pay," Ginny murmured. "I have to make him pay."

If someone had killed one of his brothers, he'd be out of his mind with rage and grief, too.

"He used to leave rose petals on my bed and in my bath," she said, her voice adopting a faraway sound as if she was trying to distance herself from the memories. "He also left a message on the mirror yesterday written in the same shade of lipstick he forced me to wear."

"Have you seen him in town?" Griff asked.

"Not exactly," she admitted. "I felt like he was following me. And when I fell the other day—"

"He pushed you?" Griff cursed. "Dammit, Ginny, why didn't you tell me?"

Emotions darkened her eyes. "Having a stalker is

not exactly something to go around bragging about. Besides, I had to make sure he was here. That real estate developer might have murdered Joy because she was the holdout on his deal."

"Jacob is looking into that angle." Griff's mind raced as he added everything up. "The dating site—you went there to try to find him." Not a question, but a statement.

"He used it once. I thought he might try again, and I could find him."

"And then what?" He clenched his hands by his sides to keep from shaking her. "Dammit, Ginny, it's too dangerous."

"Someone has to stop him," she cried. "He murdered my sister in cold blood and ruined my life." She began to pace, swinging her hands frantically. "I changed my name, my looks, everything about myself, but he's still after me."

"Your name, it isn't Ginny Bagwell?"

Regret flared in her expression. "No."

Anger railed through him. What kind of life had she lived since her sister's murder? Looking over her shoulder at every turn just as she had when he'd seen her in town. Grieving over her sister's death. Probably tormented by guilt. And fear.

This man was dangerous. *Deadly* dangerous.

"I'm sorry for what happened to you," Griff said softly. "But you can't face him alone. Let me help you."

"It's not your problem," Ginny said matter-of-factly.

Griff inched toward her, careful not to touch or push her. Now that he understood her reticence, he didn't want to frighten her.

"I'm making it my problem," Griff said. "You may have dealt with dirty or incompetent cops before, but my brothers are not them. Jacob and Liam, he's with the FBI, will find this bastard and this time he'll pay for what he did."

She rubbed her fingers over her temple, the bruise on her cheek darkening to purple. "You don't understand, Griff," Ginny said, her voice laced with panic. "I don't want you involved. He'll kill you if he thinks you're helping me."

GINNY COULDN'T LIVE with another person's death on her conscience.

"I can take care of myself," Griff said. "But we have to talk to Jacob and Liam. If this man is in town, he has to be stopped before he hurts you or someone else."

Ginny's stomach fluttered. She had to do whatever necessary to keep him from killing another woman.

Confiding in the police would throw a kink in her plan for revenge, but saving lives took priority over her own need to see him suffer.

"Tell me his name, Ginny. And if you have a picture of him, that would be helpful."

She didn't want to involve them, but she saw no choice. "I knew him as Robert Bouldercrest, but I doubt he goes by that name now. I've looked for him on social media and dating sites and Googled him, but nothing shows up."

"Liam has sources at the FBI," Griff pointed out. "What did this man do for a living?"

"Investments," she said. "That's the reason I thought he might be posing as Thad Rigden, the real estate developer. Robert used to brag that he swooped in on failing businesses and small towns, bought up the property and turned it into gold."

"But you met Rigden and it wasn't him?"

"No, it wasn't. He seemed like a cutthroat business guy, but he definitely was not Robert."

"Do you have a picture of Robert?" Griff asked.

"I'm afraid not."

"You didn't take photographs of the two of you together?" Griff sounded surprised.

"We did, but the night he tied me up, he confiscated my phone. After I escaped, I bought burner ones hoping he couldn't track me down. And when I looked up his old profile on Meet Your Mate, he'd removed it."

"How about a sketch? Can you draw one?"

"I'm not a very good artist."

"Jacob's wife, Cora, is. If you can describe him for her, she can draw a composite."

Ginny hesitated. "I don't want to involve anyone else, Griff. He might hurt them."

"Trust me, we'll take precautions. I'd never do anything to jeopardize Jacob's family."

Trust had not been part of her vocabulary for years. But Griff sounded so sincere that she relented.

"I'll call Jacob and make the arrangements. We could meet here."

"He knows I'm staying at the inn," Ginny pointed out.

"True. Then we'll go to Liam's," Griff said. "He lives out of town in the mountains. He can come here and see if Robert left prints."

"The police already have his prints," Ginny said. "And I know it's him. He left a clear message for me."

A tense second passed, then Griff phoned his brother while she found a small broom in the closet and swept up the rose petals. She cleaned the bathroom as well, then glanced at herself in the mirror. The bruise looked stark on her cheek, her eyes glassy with fear.

Hating the fact that she looked like a victim, she retrieved her purse and dabbed powder on her cheeks to cover the bruise. She finger-combed the tangles from her hair, then found Griff waiting in the entry of the room.

"We're meeting in half an hour at Liam's. Are you ready to go?"

No. She'd never be ready. She'd have to hash over her story again. Face the sympathetic faces, the condemning looks. Tell them she'd gotten her sister killed.

Hatred for Robert mounted inside her. Still, if he'd killed Joy Norris, he might kill again—before he got to her. She couldn't take the chance on not cooperating.

She riffled through her suitcase, snagged a snow cap and scarf as a disguise, then followed Griff outside to his truck. She scanned the area, and so did he, but no one seemed to be lurking around. Although Robert could be hiding in the trees behind the inn. Or in one of the cars parked on the street.

She buckled her seat belt and kept an eye out as Griff pulled onto the road leading out of town. He repeatedly checked his rearview mirror. A black sedan seemed to be following them through town as they veered to the road winding toward the mountain. But Griff sped into a side street, and the car moved on.

Tension coiled inside her as he wound up the mountain road. The sharp drop-offs, ridges and switchbacks reminded her she was living on the edge.

"Tell me about Jacob's wife," Ginny said.

Griff cleared his throat. "Her name is Cora. She was married to another man a few years ago and delivered a baby girl, but that baby was kidnapped during the hospital fire that killed my father."

Ginny released a soft gasp. "That's horrible."

"It was," he said with a sigh. "Anyway, Cora's marriage fell apart after the kidnapping, but she never gave up looking for her daughter. A few months ago, my brother reopened the case and found her little girl, so she and Cora were reunited."

"And now she's married to your brother?"

"Yep. And expecting a baby."

At least Cora's nightmare had ended. Although Ginny couldn't imagine losing a child and all the years Cora had missed with her. Memories she could never get back.

A strained silence fell between them as he drove, and he seemed deep in thought. Or maybe he was just concentrating on the road.

When they finally reached the turnoff for his brother Liam's mountain home, she realized it was isolated. The two-story log house sat at the top of a hill with a spectacular view of the mountain ridges and river. Jacob's squad car was already parked in the graveled drive.

Anxiety tightened her belly as she and Griff walked up to the house. Trees swayed in the wind, the backdrop of the mountain so scenic that her heart gave another pang. Tess would have loved it. She would have painted it with wildflowers dotting the mountains and the front yard in soft shades of colors like a watercolor palette.

Griff's brother Liam greeted them at the door and introduced himself, then Jacob introduced his wife, Cora. She was pretty and kind looking. When she laid a hand on her pregnant belly, the joy on her face was undeniable.

"Griff explained the situation. I'm sorry for what you've been through," Liam said. "I'm already talking with analysts at the Bureau to see if we can track down Bouldercrest."

The agent's direct approach was comforting. Cora gestured for her to sit on the leather sofa by the fire and offered her hot tea. Ginny accepted, grateful for the warmth to alleviate the chill that had become a permanent part of her.

"I'm so sorry for everything that's happened to you," Cora said softly. "I can't imagine."

"And I can't imagine how you suffered when your little girl was missing."

Cora smiled. "We are a pair, aren't we?"

"We are." Ginny relaxed and sipped the tea. They'd both suffered in their own way, but Cora was strong and had survived.

She would survive, too. Keeping Robert from hurting another woman was key to that survival.

HE HAD BEEN watching her for days. Mitzi was friendly. Pretty. Talked to everyone and treated each customer like a friend.

He'd seen Ginny—Reese—with her in that café. Wondered what she'd told the other woman. If she'd warned her about men like him.

Laughter sounded in his throat as he lifted the lighter and flicked it. The short flame that burst to life made his body jump with excitement. Night had fallen. Ginny had found her presents.

He'd seen her with that same man again. The firefighter.

If she thought she could hook up with some other man, she was wrong. She had to be taught another lesson.

That if she didn't come back to him, he'd just keep killing.

Let her think about that tonight when she heard about poor Mitzi.

Chapter Fourteen

Griff jammed his hands into his jeans' pockets as he glanced at Ginny. She'd been riddled with anxiety on the drive over. Who could blame her?

Her psycho ex-boyfriend had abused her, stalked her and killed her sister. All in the name of love.

No wonder she had trust issues.

Before they got started, Fletch and Jade showed up to join them, and Griff introduced everyone.

"Fletch works search and rescue on the trail," he told Ginny. "And Jade is a detective. She has connections to people in Asheville."

Ginny said hello but twisted her hands together. "I didn't realize your entire family would be here."

"Our family works together when there's a problem," Griff explained. "If your stalker is hiding out on the trail, Fletch needs to know what he looks like so he can keep an eye out. He also knows places the jerk might hide off-the-grid."

"I can't imagine Robert camping or staying in the woods," Ginny said. "He has high-class tastes."

"I'll start researching hotels and inns where he might rent a room," Jade offered.

Ginny lapsed into silence, and Cora pulled a sketch pad from a quilted shoulder bag. "Why don't we get started now?"

Griff and his brothers stepped aside and gathered around the breakfast bar where Liam had his laptop open. Jade joined them to learn the details of the case.

"I don't like the fact that she lied to you and to me," Jacob told Griff. "That she came here knowing who killed Joy and kept it to herself."

"She didn't know for certain it was him," Griff said in her defense. "How could she? It's not like he called her and admitted he killed Joy."

"She still should have come to me," Jacob said stubbornly.

Griff explained about Robert Bouldercrest bribing a cop to find her. "It took all my persuasive efforts to convince her to talk to you tonight."

Liam gave him a grim look. "I've pulled everything I could find on the Tess Taggart case. She definitely was strangled prior to the fire. There was no way Ginny could have saved her that night."

"Unless she'd stayed with Bouldercrest," Griff pointed out. "Which was not an option. Eventually he would have killed her."

"That's true," Jade cut in. "Abusers are narcissistic, obsessive and territorial. They treat women like they're possessions and have the mentality that if they can't have a woman, no one else will."

Relief tapped at Griff's mounting frustration. Protecting Ginny seemed daunting. But with his brothers' help, his tension eased slightly.

"Did she find proof that Joy was involved with this man Robert?" Liam asked.

Griff shook his head. "According to her, Joy resembled the way she used to look before she changed her appearance and went into hiding. That tipped her off to come here."

Liam turned to his computer and pulled up a photo. Griff's heart stuttered at the sight of the auburn-haired beauty on the screen. She looked young and optimistic, her green eyes glowing with happiness and the promise of a future.

"That was Ginny, aka Reese Taggart, five years ago," Liam said.

"Before she met Bouldercrest." And dyed her hair black. She must be wearing colored contacts, as well. He'd thought she was pretty when he'd met her, but she was stunning in that photograph. Had she intentionally played down her looks so as not to attract attention from Robert or any other man?

A well of sadness dug a hole in Griff's chest. What woman should have to live like that?

None. Certainly not Ginny.

Or Reese Taggart.

Anger at Robert Bouldercrest seized him. "She does resemble Joy," Griff said. Although Ginny was prettier. Sweeter. More sincere. Joy had cheated on her ex and lied to Griff.

Ginny had lied to him, but for different reasons. To protect herself.

If he'd been in her shoes, if someone he knew had killed his brothers, wouldn't he do anything to make that person pay?

"I did some checking," Jade said. "Her story about the cop being bribed to reveal her location is true. The cop who accepted that bribe has been suspended permanently. He cut a deal with the ADA to walk away quietly or face jail time."

"He could have gotten Ginny killed," Griff muttered in disgust.

Liam drummed his knuckles on the quartz countertop. "I had a feeling that if this man stalked Ginny, he might have done it before," Liam said. "I did some digging after I talked to Jacob and found another homicide investigation with a similar MO. This one was in Savannah, Georgia."

Griff went bone still. "Ginny wasn't his first victim?"

Liam shook his head. "I don't think so. I think we're dealing with a serial predator. And he's not going to stop until we catch him."

GINNY FELT A kinship with Cora that reminded her of her relationship with Tess.

She described Robert in detail, correcting Cora when she drew the mouth a little too wide and the eyes too slanted. His nose was more narrow, chin had a cleft. Robert hadn't looked evil in the least. He could have been a model for an entrepreneurial magazine or *GQ*.

"Nothing about him stood out as abnormal or dangerous," she told Cora. "Not until you crossed him."

"That's the worst kind," Cora said softly. "And the easiest to fall for."

"I was such a fool," Ginny said in a raw whisper.

Cora squeezed her hand. "This man was a predator, so don't blame yourself. You were trusting and had no reason to suspect he wasn't who he pretended to be. That's the nature of a sociopath. Just look at Charles Manson and all the women he charmed."

"But my sister died because I wore blinders," Ginny said in a raw whisper.

Cora squeezed her hand in understanding. "I'm sure she wouldn't blame you, and she wouldn't want you to blame yourself."

Probably true. Tess was selfless, full of life. Optimistic to a fault. And as trusting as Ginny had been.

She missed her so much her heart gave a pang.

Cora finished the sketch and turned it to face Ginny. "Is this close?"

Perspiration beaded on Ginny's neck at the sheer likeness of the drawing to Robert's face. "That's him."

Jade joined them and studied the photo. "We'll pass this to all local law authorities and issue an APB for him."

"He probably altered his appearance now. He knows the police are still looking for him in connection to my sister's murder and is like a chameleon. He fits in wherever he is and goes unnoticed."

Jade's determined expression didn't waver. "Don't worry. The Maverick men are smart, thorough and determined. They'll find him."

Cora squeezed Ginny's hand. "You can trust us. This family takes care of each other."

"Liam and Jacob are two of the finest lawmen I've ever known," Jade continued. "And Fletch..." A warm smile flickered in her eyes as she glanced at her husband. "He's honest and trustworthy and will do everything he can to track down this man."

"I...don't know what to say," Ginny whispered. "The lawmen I worked with before treated me like what happened was my fault." If she remembered correctly, they'd treated her mother as a suspect when her father was first murdered, too.

"I understand how it feels to be looked at with suspicion," Cora said. "When my daughter was kidnapped, the police acted as if my husband, at the time, and I did something to her. It was a horrible feeling and made me not want to work with the police."

Ginny wiped her clammy hands on her slacks. Cora did understand.

"And I know what it's like to be a victim," Jade added. "A few months ago, I was investigating a serial murder case when I was attacked and left for dead in the mountains in the middle of a blizzard. When I came to, I didn't remember my name or what happened."

Ginny gaped at her. "How did you survive?"

Jade smiled. "Fletch found me and carried me to a shelter to wait out the storm. Slowly my memories started to return. But I had nightmares for weeks afterward." She gestured toward Jacob and Liam. "Those men saved my life and helped me seek justice." Sincerity laced her voice. "They'll help you, too, Ginny. You just have to trust them."

A warmth seeped through Ginny, chasing away some of the chill. Both of these women had overcome trauma and seemed stronger for it. Could she do the same?

Jade reached for the sketch. "Let me give this to Liam so he can log it into the system."

Cora handed her the sketch and Jade passed it to the men. Griff scrutinized the sketch, then walked over to her with a grim expression. He probably wondered how she could have been so gullible to have entangled herself with a sadistic psycho like Robert.

She'd asked herself the same question a thousand times.

"Let me make some more tea." Cora excused herself and went to the kitchen.

Griff slid onto the sofa beside Ginny. "You okay?" he asked softly.

She nodded, although nothing about this situation was okay. "I can't believe I allowed this to happen."

"Don't do that," Griff said firmly. "Stop blaming yourself for being a victim."

"That's hard to do when my sister lost her life because of me."

A tense silence lingered for a moment before Griff spoke. "You weren't the only one who fell for him."

Ginny wrinkled her brow. "You mean Joy?"

Griff shrugged. "No. There was another woman before you. At least Liam found a victim who fit the same profile. She was from Savannah, Georgia."

Ginny's heart stuttered. "She was strangled?"

"And her house set on fire," Griff said. "Her name was Ava Frances. She was twenty-five. Her coworkers said she met a man on a dating site. His name was David Lakin. He was an investor."

"Just like Robert," Ginny said in a low voice.

Griff nodded. "One of her friends apparently became suspicious of his behavior. After they were engaged, Ava pulled away from her friends and family, even left her job to stay home and be the wife he wanted."

Goose bumps skated up Ginny's arms. "What happened?"

"One of the girlfriends confronted him, and he strangled her and burned down her apartment with her in it."

Oh, God. Images of Tess's dead body taunted Ginny. She thought she was going to be sick.

"A week later, the fiancée ended up dead, strangled and left in her car which he set on fire."

Ginny leaned forward with her elbows on her knees, lowered her head and took several deep breaths to stem the nausea.

Robert had done the same thing to another woman before her, and he'd killed her friend just like he had Tess. Who knows how many more women's lives he would destroy if they didn't stop him now?

He hadn't left any of his lovers, witnesses or anyone who'd crossed him alive.

Which meant he didn't want her as his wife as he'd said. He wanted to kill her.

Now that Griff understood the reason Ginny was running and her distrust of the police, her actions made sense. Hopefully, Cora and Jade had alleviated her anxiety over confiding in him and his brothers.

"Bouldercrest knows where Ginny's staying?" Jacob asked.

Griff nodded. "He's been in her room at the inn."

"Did she report the break-in to the innkeeper?"

"I don't think so. After what happened with that dirty cop, I don't think she's trusted anyone since."

Griff wanted her to trust him almost as much as he wanted to protect her.

"I can assign a car outside the inn," Jacob suggested. "If he shows up there, we'll grab him."

"Good. Although I don't think Ginny should stay at the inn tonight," Griff said. "It's too dangerous."

Jacob arched a brow. "What do you suggest?"

"She can stay in my spare room. My security system is state-of-the-art."

"True," Liam said. "Although if this guy saw you with Ginny, it could be dangerous for you."

Griff squared his shoulders. "I can handle myself. You forget I face danger every day on the job."

"This is different," Jacob said. "You aren't just dealing with an arsonist. This is a cold-blooded psychopath."

"All the more reason we make sure he doesn't get to Ginny," Griff said.

His brothers reluctantly agreed, and Jacob phoned his deputy about standing guard at the inn in case Bouldercrest showed. Liam scanned the sketch Cora had drawn of the man and entered it into the system to alert law-enforcement agencies to be on the lookout for him. Fletch took a copy to pass to the rangers on the AT and to use as a reference himself.

"Anything more on the teens and the wildfire arsons?" he asked Jacob.

"I don't think those boys are the perps. My guess is the arsonist saw where the boys had been partying in the woods and started the fires close by, assuming we'd instantly accuse the teens."

"Which we did," Griff muttered. "What if Bouldercrest set the fires to distract us from Joy's murder and from Ginny?"

"That's possible," Liam agreed.

Jacob patted Griff's back. "Don't let down your guard, man. Bouldercrest has gotten away with four murders so far that we know of, and an attempt on Ginny's life. He's smart and methodical."

GRIFF PROMISED TO be careful and call Jacob if he noticed any sign Robert was following him. Cora and Jade gave Ginny a hug of encouragement before they left, and Griff's heart squeezed with affection for his sisters-in-law. His family had always come together in a crisis and were doing so now. He was a lucky man to have them.

Ginny was alone and had nobody. He couldn't let her down.

"We're going to find him and bring him to justice," Griff assured her as he drove to his cabin.

Ginny stared out the truck window. "I hope so. He's destroyed enough lives already."

He didn't know how to respond. She was right. It was her reality. But he had the sudden urge to pull her in his arms and assure her that no one would ever hurt her again.

She'd balked at the idea of staying at his place, but he insisted. "We should stop at the inn and let me pack a bag."

He shook his head. "Not tonight. He might be watching, and I don't want him to follow us to my place. I'll drive you back in the morning."

A sliver of fear flashed in her eyes. Was she afraid to spend the night at his cabin?

"Ginny, I swear you'll have your own room and privacy at my house. I have a state-of-the-art security system so no one can get in. And I won't bother you."

"Robert had a security system, too. He used it to keep me locked inside."

Griff inhaled a sharp breath. "I'm not him," he said, anger toward the monster who'd abused her throbbing inside him. "I just want you to be safe for the night. Jacob is stationing his deputy outside the inn, so if Robert shows up there tonight, we might catch him and this nightmare will be over."

She shivered and dug herself deeper inside her jacket as if the thin coat could hold the demons at bay.

He hoped she didn't see him as one of them.

Chapter Fifteen

In spite of Griff's reassurances, Ginny insisted he stop by and let her pick up her car. Call it a safety net, but it was important that she be able to come and go of her own free will. She would never let another man dictate her life or trap her again.

Griff didn't like the idea of going anywhere near the inn, but he agreed to a compromise and asked Jacob to have one of the deputies drop her car at his house. She'd been alone so long now that she'd forgotten what it was like not to be alone.

To have a family, people who came together and supported you when you needed it. People who'd literally do anything for you. Griff had that with his brothers. They obviously shared affection for each other and worked together.

What would it be like to have a family like that?

You had it with Tess. Except you let Robert alienate you from her.

Her lungs squeezed with her need for air. Griff parked in front of his log cabin, and she realized how much he must love these mountains and the town to have stayed after his father's death. She and Tess sold their family home after they lost their mother. It had been too painful to go inside the rooms where they'd grown up. Every place she'd turned she'd seen her parents, childhood memories, the love. The emptiness. That void had been overpowering.

"You must be tired," Griff said as they battled the wind up to his front porch. "How's your head?"

"I'm fine." Although she winced at the reminder of her encounter with her attacker. If Robert had jumped her, he would have said something to let her know if it was him, wouldn't he? Maybe she had angered Thad Rigden.

But he seemed too sophisticated to assault a woman in an alley.

"Your house is beautiful," she said as they entered. "It feels warm and cozy."

"Thanks," Griff said. "After we lost our folks, we decided to sell the old homestead and each of us built a cabin. It was too hard going back to the house."

Ginny smiled. "Tess and I sold our parents' home after my mom passed, too." Another thing they had in common.

Griff flipped a switch and the gas logs in the fireplace burst to life. The floor-to-ceiling stone fireplace and rustic features added charm, and the picture window and French doors leading to the massive deck offered a beautiful scenic view. Soft firelight flickered and danced, adding warmth and an ambience that would have been romantic if romance was part of her life.

"Did you do some of the work yourself?" she asked as she admired the millwork and rustic mantel.

"Yeah, it's kind of a hobby. I built the bannister and made my table out of reclaimed wood." Pride filled his voice. "And the columns were made from heart pine from my parents' property."

Impressive. "It's lovely that you brought a piece of history with you."

"My brothers and I all did."

Just like she'd kept the quilt her grandmother had made for her and carried it with her wherever she moved.

Griff set the alarm system, then offered her a drink. "I have whiskey or wine," he said.

"A whiskey would be great." And alleviate some of her anxiety.

He poured them both a finger in a highball glass, then handed it to her. She swirled the liquid around in the glass while he began pulling items from the refrigerator.

"I hope you like omelets," he said. "My specialty for dinner when I haven't grocery shopped."

"I hadn't thought about dinner," she admitted as she crossed the room to stare out the French doors. The trees shivered in the breeze, and stars fought through the storm clouds but failed, pitching the night into almost total darkness.

Exactly the way she'd felt for three years.

She glanced back at Griff, and her stomach fluttered. Before she'd been scarred and broken, she would have been attracted to him. Heck, she still was.

But she didn't belong here. Not in his home or with his family.

She didn't belong anywhere anymore.

GRIFF ADDED ONIONS, peppers and mushrooms to the pan, then watched them sizzle in olive oil until they softened before he stirred in the eggs and added cheese. The scent of bacon frying on his griddle made his mouth water.

He needed to distract himself from thinking about Ginny in his kitchen. As she stood by his window gazing at the inky sky and mountain ranges, she looked tormented. He loved the seclusion of the mountains and wilderness but considering Ginny's situation, he understood her wariness. Although for a moment, he'd seen longing in her expression, as if she wanted to be part of this beautiful place.

As if she was all alone.

He'd never thought about being lonely before himself, because he had his brothers. Although there were all kinds of lonely.

Two of his brothers had partners now, lovers and wives. He envied them. And tonight, sharing a simple meal with Ginny in his cabin felt intimate.

A self-deprecating sigh escaped him. He could not entertain fantasies about a relationship with her. For God's sake, she was a domestic violence victim with a stalker.

Anger at the situation and the bastard heated his blood and made him renew his vow to protect her.

He dished up the omelets and bacon, then grabbed toast from the toaster and set strawberry jam on the table. "It's ready," he said, wondering what she'd think of his culinary skills.

She turned and looked so vulnerable that his gut instinct whispered for him to sweep her in his arms and hold her until her fear subsided.

Don't do it. The exact worst thing he could do was to touch her.

"It smells delicious," she said as she joined him at the breakfast bar.

"Another whiskey?" he offered.

She shook her head. "I need to keep my wits about me in case Robert finds us."

Dammit, no woman should have to think like that.

He pushed the whiskey bottle to the back of the bar and filled glasses of water for them. He needed to stay alert himself. If this maniac found her here, he'd tear his damn head off. Then he'd call his brothers.

She seated herself at the counter, and he dropped onto the stool beside her, careful not to crowd her.

"You didn't have to do this," she said as she reached for her fork.

"I had to eat," he said. "Besides, I enjoy being in the kitchen. At the firehouse, we take turns cooking."

A smile softened her eyes. "My mother enjoyed cooking, too. She said it relaxed her."

He grinned. "Chopping vegetables is cathartic." A good way to release tension.

She smiled again, and he realized he'd been chopping ever since they returned to his place. He had to keep his damn hands busy so he wouldn't touch her.

"So, your mother liked to cook?" he asked to fill the awkward silence.

"She did." She forked up a bite full of the omelet and devoured it. "Delicious. Did you use fresh chives?"

"I did," Griff said. "You know your herbs?"

"Mom again. She was on a low-salt diet, so she substituted fresh herbs instead."

"Did she have a specialty?"

"Pasta dishes and desserts," Ginny said. "She treated pastries like an art form just like my sister did when she painted."

"Your sister was an artist?"

"Watercolor was her favorite medium," Ginny said thoughtfully. "She painted beautiful landscapes with vibrant reds and oranges and subtle blues and greens. She would have wanted to paint your view out back."

Griff allowed them to sit in the moment as she remembered her sister and they ate. "I can't imagine living anywhere but here on the mountain."

"I can't imagine being able to settle down," she admitted softly. "The past three years I haven't stayed in the same place for more than three or four months. I'd get nervous and feel like I was being watched, then move on to the next town."

Griff's stomach clenched. "That must be difficult," he murmured. Even after his father and mother passed, he still had family left. Ginny had no one.

A strained silence fell as they finished their meal. When she stood to clear the dishes, he shook his head. "I've got it. Go get some rest. It's been a long day."

She paused at the edge of the breakfast bar and looked up at him with a dozen emotions in her eyes. "Why are you being so nice to me? I lied to you. I…got my sister killed and may have gotten Joy killed, too."

Griff couldn't resist. He lifted his hands and gently rubbed her arms. "You did lie, but I understand the reason now. And you are not responsible for your sister's death or Joy's." He didn't know how to convince her to believe him. "This guy is a manipulator, Ginny.

You saw what he wanted you to see. Once you realized who and what he was, you did what you had to do."

"But my sweet sister is dead because of it," Ginny said.

Griff squeezed her arm. "Your sister would have wanted you to leave an abusive situation." He lowered his voice. "She'd also want you to be happy now, too."

"I can't be happy as long as he's out there." She ran her fingers through her hair, then turned and walked into the guest bedroom.

A minute later, he heard her lock the door and the room went dark.

GINNY CURLED BENEATH the thick quilt in Griff's extra bedroom and listened to the wind beat at the roof and windows. March had swept in with a vengeance, keeping winter alive in the mountains and a foreboding chill in the air that lingered like the coldness in her heart.

For just a minute today, surrounded by Griff's loving family and the compassion of the two wives, she'd almost felt a crack in the veneer. Had almost felt like there might be a possibility for a future for her without a maniac breathing down her neck.

That there might a light at the end of the dark tunnel she'd fallen into when she'd held her lifeless sister in her arms.

She shivered and burrowed deeper beneath the quilt, wondering what hands had lovingly stitched the log-cabin pattern. In addition to baking, her mother had loved quilting and so had her grandmother. When she was a little girl, she remembered sitting in her grandma's sewing room while she spread colorful swatches of dozens of fabrics across her worktable. Although Tess had been the artist, she'd enjoyed helping her grandma arrange the different swatches and colors into a design.

One year Grammy pieced quilts for her and Tess as Christmas gifts. They'd slept curled beneath them on cold winter nights and pretended their grandma's arms were lovingly wrapped around them. The quilts had become even more special after she'd passed.

Footsteps echoed from the living room, and she tensed, holding her breath the way she used to do when she heard Robert come home. Would he be in a loving mood? Demand her attention? Or would he be angry and vent his frustration on her? Had she done something to incense him? Had she left a glass on the counter? Forgotten to stack the dishes the way he'd taught her?

Forgotten to fold the afghan across the couch? Left the magazines scattered instead of stacked in alphabetical order?

She clutched the quilt edge, listening for the footsteps to grow closer. For the doorknob to jiggle.

But instead, they faded. Griff was out there, not Robert. Griff who'd promised to protect her.

Would she ever be able to enjoy intimacy with a man again?

The memory of Griff pulling her into his arms taunted her. It had felt so…good. Tender. Unlike Robert's possessive brute force.

She hated him for changing her. For ruining her trust and for making her skeptical of every man she met.

The anxiety inside her spread, and she curled lower beneath the bedding, savoring the warmth and comfort it offered. The house was quiet, the faint glow of a quarter moon seeping through the dark storm clouds and glowing gently in the room.

Exhausted from the attack, she closed her eyes and allowed herself to drift asleep.

In her dreams, she wasn't broken anymore. And the world was full of colors.

GRIFF STOOD OUTSIDE on his deck, counting his blessings and wrangling unwanted feelings for Ginny under control.

She deserved better. True happiness and relief from the suffocating burden of guilt weighing her down.

Damn, he wanted to fix all her problems. That meant protecting her, and helping his brothers track down the man who'd made her life miserable.

He gazed at the heavens, willing his father to send him strength and his mother her wisdom. Something rustled in the woods behind his house, and he tensed and scanned the trees. Hard to see much of anything at night. The moonlight barely created a dent in the darkness, and somewhere in the distance, a coyote howled.

He reached inside his den and snagged his night binoculars from the side table by the sofa, then returned and used them to scan the property. Leaves rustled and tree branches swayed in the wind.

His protective instincts for Ginny mounted as he pictured Robert Bouldercrest skulking around trying to frighten her. What kind of lowlife coward preyed on women and enjoyed their fear?

He'd never understand that kind of evil.

Senses alert, he kept watch for another hour. Finally, when he was satisfied the bastard was gone, if he was out there, he closed the door and locked it. Then he checked to verify that the security system was armed, shuffled into his bedroom and stripped down to his boxers. After he brushed his teeth, he climbed in bed.

But just as he closed his eyes to grab a few hours of sleep, his phone buzzed. He snatched it from his nightstand. His chief.

"Griff, we need you. A fire in town. Burgess just came down with some kind of bug and is puking his guts out. And Thomas sprained his damn ankle on the last job."

Griff sat up and instantly reached for his clothes. "Where's the fire?"

"Mitzi's Café."

His feet hit the floor. Would Ginny be safe if he left her here with the security system armed?

Chapter Sixteen

Griff hated to wake Ginny. But he didn't want to leave without alerting her that he'd be gone.

He quickly dressed, then checked out the windows again. Nothing seemed amiss, so he knocked on the guest-bedroom door. "Ginny?"

Except for the wind battering the house, everything seemed quiet. He waited a couple more minutes, then knocked again. "Ginny, it's Griff. I have to go."

Footsteps shuffled from inside the room, then he heard the lock turn and the door opened a fraction of an inch. Ginny looked up at him through sleep-glazed eyes. Her hair was tousled, her face void of makeup, making her look young and innocent and so beautiful his chest clenched. Although the bruise on her cheek reminded him that she was in danger.

"What's wrong?" she asked, her tone confused as if he'd woken her from a deep sleep.

"There's a fire in town," he said. "I have to go. I just wanted you to know where I was if you woke up and I wasn't back."

She blinked, her brow pinched. "A fire?"

"Yeah. In town. Mitzi's diner." He hesitated. "Go

back to bed. I'll set the alarm. You'll be safe here for the night."

"Mitzi's? But I was just there."

"I know. It was probably just a kitchen fire, but the team is short and needs me. The security system is synced with my phone, and you have my number. Lock the bedroom door again and go back to sleep. I'll be back as soon as possible."

She gave a little nod although she looked troubled by the thought of another fire. He didn't want to frighten her, but his own mind had gone to a dark place. Mitzi was single and lived alone. It was possible Robert could have targeted her as another victim.

He waited until she closed the door and the lock turned before he checked the security system. He grabbed his jacket and phone on the way out the door, then scanned his property before he climbed in his truck. Even as he started the engine, he surveyed the periphery and woods beyond in case Robert had discovered that Ginny had come to his house.

The road was deserted, the forest quiet, no lights burning in the darkness to raise suspicion. Once he hit the main road, he sped up and made it to town in record time. The guys from his station house were already on the scene, rolling out hoses and gearing up.

The fire looked somewhat contained to the back of the café where the kitchen was located. It was late so Mitzi would have gone home already.

He dashed to the truck, found an extra uniform and mask and geared up to go in.

"Any word on Mitzi?" he asked as he hurried over to Baxter who was in charge and doling out orders.

"No, but we just arrived."

"Who called it in?"

"Don't know," Baxter said. "There's the sheriff. Maybe he knows."

Jacob jogged over to him. "Didn't realize you were working tonight, Griff," Jacob said.

"Squad needed me. I'll check and see if anyone's inside. Find out if Mitzi is home and if she's all right."

"On it." Jacob patted his arm. "Be careful, bro."

Griff nodded, yanked his oxygen mask over his face and ran toward the burning building. Smoke billowed in a thick cloud, clogging his vision, but the front of the café hadn't yet caught. The scent of burning wood and metal was strong, and he scanned the room, but it was empty.

"Anyone here?" The crackling of wood and hissing of the blaze was the only response. Mitzi or even the janitor could be in the back, trapped or hurt. He dodged a patch of flames as he wove past the tables and through the door leading to the kitchen. When he opened the door, flames danced along the back wall.

He glanced at the gas stove and wondered if that had been the source of the fire. Had Mitzi left it on by accident?

Behind him, his men moved in. They began to douse the flames and he scanned the room, searching. "Mitzi? Anyone in here?"

No answer.

He inched around the wood cabinet by the pantry door and the entrance to the small office. A piece of burning board splintered down, and he knocked it away with gloved hands then plowed around another patch of flames. He shone his flashlight in the pantry and yelled again, but there was no one inside. The bags of flour and sugar and other food products were erupting as he stepped back to check the office.

Cookbooks and menu guides filled a shelf above the desk where a computer sat along with other stacks of papers. Thankfully the office was empty.

They worked for over an hour to extinguish and contain the blaze. Sweat beaded Griff's neck. He tasted ash as he finished up and searched for an accelerant. An empty lighter-fluid can lay in the corner of the kitchen near the stove.

Arson.

He asked Baxter to bag it for evidence and to look for other forensics once the embers died down and they could search more thoroughly.

With Ginny on his mind, he checked his phone. No word from her. Jacob had texted though.

Mitzi is not home. Looks like there was a scuffle. Blood on the floor. I think she was taken.

Griff's blood ran cold, and he ran to tell Baxter that he had to go. Then he jumped in his car and headed toward Mitzi's.

GINNY WAS SO exhausted she fell back asleep immediately. Being in Griff's house had lulled her into a sense of security she hadn't felt in years.

But an hour later, she woke with a start. A noise outside? Someone lurking at the window?

Grabbing her gun from her purse and her phone

from the nightstand, she eased open the curtains. She peered outside, her breathing ragged.

On first perusal, no one was visible. But that didn't mean someone wasn't out there.

Fear knifing through her, she tiptoed to the bedroom door, pressed her ear to the wood and listened. No voices or footsteps. Her chest eased slightly. Griff had said he'd set the alarm, but Robert was tech savvy. If there was a way to disarm it, he'd find it.

She had to check the house before she could totally relax again. Griff's words drifted through her consciousness. A fire in town. Mitzi's diner.

She'd eaten at Mitzi's. Had talked to the pretty young woman. Had questioned other people in the diner.

What if Robert had been watching? What if the fire at the café was his way of getting her attention? Or… what if he'd seen her being friendly with the woman and decided to hurt Mitzi to punish *her*?

Fear squeezed at her lungs, robbing her breath. No…not Mitzi…not another woman hurt because of her.

Anger compounded her fear, and she clenched her gun, then eased open the lock on the bedroom door. Griff had left a light on in the kitchen, illuminating it in a soft glow. The curtains were drawn over the French doors. The front door closed.

No sign anyone was inside.

Still, Robert could be lurking somewhere on the property. With acres of woods, there were dozens of places to hide. Or he could be with Mitzi, playing one of his mind games or physically hurting her before he…killed her.

Choking back a cry, she eased into the room and scanned the space. Just as it had been when she'd gone to bed. She inched toward the French doors, holding her breath with every step. When she reached the curtain, she summoned her courage and gently pushed it aside just an inch to look out into the forest.

A tree branch snapped off in the wind. Storm clouds rumbled. A few feet into the woods and she thought she spotted a light. Just a tiny pinpoint, no bigger than the point of a sewing needle.

A cigarette? A lighter?

Heart racing, she blinked to clear her vision and narrowed her eyes. Yes, there it was. A small light flickering against the darkness.

And it was moving. Coming closer.

Her hands trembled. Her legs felt weak. But Tess's face flashed behind her eyes, and she raised her gun. *Come on, Robert. I'm waiting. If you're out there, just try getting to me.*

She steeled herself as she watched the light move closer and closer and closer. Then it was in the backyard.

She glanced down at her phone for a millisecond. Considered calling Griff.

There was no time. She had to handle this herself. Get rid of Robert forever.

GRIFF THREW THE truck into Park in front of Mitzi's.

Jacob's police car was parked in the drive, the lights

in the house's interior shining. He hit the ground at a fast walk, then knocked at the door. "It's me, Jacob."

Jacob met him at the door. "Don't touch anything. I called for an Evidence Response Team to process the house. If Ginny's stalker kidnapped Mitzi, we have to follow the book. Any evidence we collect might help put him away."

"Got it." Griff wiped a hand over his sweaty hair. "I think the fire at Mitzi's was arson. We found a can of lighter fluid in the kitchen. He probably turned on the gas stove and lit up the place."

"How much damage?" Jacob asked.

"Mostly the kitchen and her office. Except for smoke and water damage, the front dining room is okay." If they found Mitzi and she was safe, she could rebuild.

He just prayed she was alive.

Jacob gestured for Griff to follow him. Griff avoided touching the walls or doorway or anything inside. The living area looked undisturbed, lamps and bookshelves and furnishings neatly kept. Cookbooks lined an open shelf beside the window that overlooked the backyard in the kitchen. A collection of pottery in a dusty green color filled one shelf, and a coffee station occupied a corner. A large island with a stainless steel counter completed the room, a cook's dream. Even the kitchen towels were lined up neatly and evenly on the towel rack on the side of the island.

"Everything looks intact," he commented.

"Until you reach the bedroom," Jacob pointed out. "That's another reason to suspect foul play. She seems particular about her belongings but look in here."

Jacob gestured to the open doorway into the bedroom, and Griff understood what he meant. The bedding was not only rumpled, but twisted and torn off the bed, dangling as if Mitzi had fought with someone. The bedside lamp was overturned, the glass base shattered. Blood dotted the floor beside it.

Had she grabbed it to defend herself?

Or had her abductor cut himself?

Jacob pointed to the rustic pine floor and the floral rug at the foot of the brass bed. More blood. "Looks like they fought, and he dragged her from the bed. Whoever was cut bled, but it's not a significant amount, so hopefully Mitzi's still alive."

"But for how long?" Griff grumbled.

"If we can match the blood type or DNA to Bouldercrest, we can confirm we're dealing with the same perp." Jacob narrowed his eyes. "Do you know if Mitzi was seeing anyone?"

"I have no idea," Griff said. "But her coworkers at the café might."

Jacob heaved a breath. "I'll canvass her neighbors and talk to her staff."

Griff glanced into the bathroom. It was just as neat as the other room. Whatever had happened had occurred in the bedroom.

A sick feeling knotted his stomach. The protective order Ginny had issued against Bouldercrest had failed. Griff stiffened his spine.

He would not fail her.

"If Robert abducted Mitzi, why set the fire at her café instead of her house?" he asked.

Jacob furrowed his brows. "To divide our manpower. We need people investigating here and at the café."

"Smart." Another thought occurred to Griff. "If he discovered Ginny is with me, he might want to lure me away." God. And it had worked.

"I have to get back to Ginny." He could call but he hoped she was sleeping and safe and sound.

"I have to wait on the ERT," Jacob said. "But if you get there and see him, call me for backup." Jacob pressed a hand to Griff's chest. "This guy is dangerous, Griff. Don't try to take him down yourself."

He wasn't a weakling. If Bouldercrest was there and threatening Ginny, he'd do whatever necessary to protect her.

"You will call me, won't you?" Jacob asked in the big brother tone he'd used to order him around when he was a kid. Jacob still thought it would work.

He almost laughed, but simply nodded. He didn't have time to argue. If Robert had kidnapped Mitzi, she was in danger. Jacob needed to work on finding her.

And if the bastard had set the fire to lure Griff away and divide law enforcement, he might be at Griff's place now.

Heart pounding, he hurried through the house and outside to his truck. He fired up the engine, tires squealing as he raced from her driveway and sped toward home.

Traffic was practically nonexistent in the middle of the night, except for a couple of truckers, and he maneuvered around them and wove onto the winding road to his cabin. With every mile, his fear intensified.

If Bouldercrest had kidnapped Mitzi, where would

he take her? Would he kill her right away or keep her for his own sick pleasure? Where would he hide out?

Poor Mitzi. She was an innocent in all this. She didn't deserve to be hurt or used as a pawn in a demented man's twisted game. And she certainly didn't deserve to die.

Neither did Ginny.

His phone buzzed. The alarm company. He snatched it and connected.

"Your alarm has been activated. You have ninety seconds to turn it off or 9-1-1 will be alerted."

Someone had triggered the alarm. He had to get to Ginny…

GINNY FROZE AT the sound of the alarm trilling.

She'd been staring at the backyard. The light was gone. No…on the steps. Moving upward.

Her hand wobbled. She pressed her finger over the trigger. Aimed.

Suddenly a loud noise startled her. Something hit the glass in the French doors. Instead of breaking, they rattled.

Then she saw Robert. His face pressed against the glass.

Chapter Seventeen

Griff barreled up the mountain road to his cabin, scanning the road and woods for any signs of Ginny's stalker. He phoned the security company and asked them to hold off on a police car, that he was almost home.

If he needed one, he'd call Jacob.

Darkness bathed the forest, night sounds echoing in the wilderness offering endless places for a predator to hide. His headlights caught sight of an animal in the road. A stray dog. He swerved to avoid running over it, tires churning on the graveled embankment until he righted his truck. Another mile, and he sped up his driveway.

No sign of trouble as he approached. The light in the guest room was off. Only the soft glow of the kitchen light above the window shone. He couldn't see his deck from the front, but he didn't spot a car or other vehicle on the property. But Bouldercrest could have come up from the woods or the river. Canoes and other small boats traveled behind the property and could put in at any number of docks or places along the way.

He flipped off his lights, not wanting to alert

Bouldercrest if he was waiting in ambush. He slowed and parked in front of the house, then reached inside the dash of his truck and removed his pistol. A second later, he threw open the door, eased along the bushes toward his porch then climbed the steps as quietly as possible.

When he reached the porch landing, he peered through the window to the side. The light in the kitchen was still on, the fire in the fireplace glowing. Everything seemed still. Quiet. No movement.

Holding his breath, he punched in the security code to quiet it, then unlocked the door and eased into the entryway. He inched toward the living area/kitchen, keeping his gun by his side and ready.

Just as he passed the bench by the front door, he glanced toward the guest-bedroom door. It was open. Where was Ginny?

Heart hammering again, he crept toward the living room and scanned it. His pulse jumped when he finally spotted her. She was crouched behind the big club chair, a gun poised and aimed at him, her eyes wide and startled looking. Even in the shadows, he could feel waves of fear rolling off her.

"Ginny," he threw up his hands in warning. "Don't shoot. It's Griff."

Her hand trembled in the firelight, but she didn't budge. "Ginny, listen. It's me. The alarm went off and I came back to check on you." He stowed his gun in the back of his jeans, then reached out his hand and slowly moved toward her.

"You're safe now. Please put the gun down," he said

in a low, soothing voice. Another step, another inch. Her breathing rattled in the tense silence.

"Look at me," he murmured. "It's me, Griff."

She blinked then his face must have finally registered, because she lowered her hand and let her gun hang to her side. He hurried toward her, knelt in front of her and eased the weapon from her hand where she was still clenching it.

His jaw tightened as he desperately tried to control his rage. He didn't like any stranger on his property, especially one who preyed on women.

"You're safe," he whispered as he cupped her face between his hands and forced her to look into his eyes.

"No," she said, her voice cracking. "He was here. He was outside. I saw him."

GINNY THOUGHT SHE could handle facing Robert, but she'd frozen up when she'd seen his sinister face through the window.

Dammit, she had to figure out a way to get the upper hand. Not to let him paralyze her.

"He was here?" Griff asked. "Where?"

"Out back. I saw a cigarette burning. Then movement. He crossed the backyard and just walked up onto the deck."

"Bold move." Griff rubbed her arms gently. "You're sure. You saw his face?"

She murmured *yes*. "He threw something against the French doors. It banged the glass."

"Did he try to break in?"

"No," she whispered. "The alarm was blaring, and he just smiled…then disappeared."

Griff frowned.

"He likes to play games," Ginny explained. "Taunt me. He did it before. Wanted to show me he could get close to me without being caught."

A tense second passed. "Let me see what he threw at the glass." He walked over to the doors.

Ginny followed him, anxious to know if Robert had really left or if he was lurking in the shadows. Maybe he thought she'd check outside to see what he'd thrown, and he'd snatch her.

Griff pushed the curtain aside and peered through the darkness, scanning the deck.

But he didn't see anyone. The woods were thick with trees and night shadows though, so it was possible he was still watching.

Although why hide in the woods when he'd accomplished his goal? If he'd wanted to attack her or hurt her tonight, he would have broken in when he was on the deck.

Griff unlocked the door, opened it and stepped outside. Ginny hugged the doorjamb and kept her eyes peeled for an attack while he shone a flashlight across the deck. His body tensed as he knelt. Then he pulled a handkerchief from his pocket, wrapped it around his hand and used it to pick up something on the deck floor.

"What is it?" Ginny asked as he stepped back inside.

Griff opened his palm and her pulse jumped. At first sight, it appeared to simply be one of the smooth river rocks. But as he spread his fingers, she noticed a piece of paper wrapped around it. Griff eased away the rubber band holding it in place, revealing a strand of hair.

"Oh, my God. Is that what I think it is?" she asked in a raw whisper.

"I think so." He angled the note for her to read it, and her stomach churned.

Mitzi says hello. Don't make me kill her.

GRIFF STARED AT the message in silence. He'd never met Robert Bouldercrest, but he hated the creep. He was not only dangerous, but he was downright cruel.

"He has Mitzi," Ginny said, her voice hoarse with emotions. She grabbed his arm. "Did you know, Griff?"

He made a low sound in his throat. "I wasn't sure," he said. "She wasn't at the café where the fire began. Jacob went to her house to look for her, but she was gone."

"Gone?"

"It looks like there was a struggle in her bedroom." He closed the door and locked it again. He drew the curtains, blocking out the sightline of the mountains and woods where Robert had been skulking.

But the message on that damn rock was imprinted on his brain. And Mitzi's hair…what had he done to her? Was there still time to save her? If so, how?

Ginny looked frightened and angry at the same time. He couldn't blame her.

"Let me call Jacob," Griff said. "He needs to put this stone into evidence and verify the hair belongs to Mitzi. And Liam can get people searching the area for Bouldercrest."

Ginny's voice warbled. "He wants to torture me by making me imagine the evil things he's doing to her."

Griff muttered a curse. The man was an animal. And he knew Mitzi was with him now.

Griff rubbed her arms again. "Sit by the fire and warm up."

She sank onto the chair and dropped her head into her hands as he phoned Jacob. "I'm still at Mitzi's with the ERT," Jacob said. "What's going on?"

Griff explained about Robert's visit and the gift he'd left for Ginny. "She's certain it's him, and that he has Mitzi. We need to find her fast, Jacob."

"I'll call Liam. We'll get men combing the woods behind your house and set up roadblocks."

"He's not trying to get out of town," Griff muttered in disgust. "He wants to torment Ginny by keeping Mitzi close by."

"You're right. I'll organize a search team with the volunteer deputies in the county," Jacob said. "They can start searching abandoned buildings and cabins in the area. Bouldercrest has to be holed up somewhere. And we're damn well going to find him."

But would they do that before he killed Mitzi? Griff chewed the inside of his cheek to keep from voicing his concern out loud. He certainly didn't want to in front of Ginny. She was in enough agony already.

"I'll stop by in the morning to pick up the stone to send to the lab," Jacob said. "Meanwhile you'd better stay there with Ginny. And keep your alarm system armed."

"Don't worry. I won't leave her alone again." He didn't intend to allow Bouldercrest to get to her on his watch.

THE PROTECTIVENESS IN Griff's voice warmed Ginny and helped to soothe her frayed nerves. Although anxiety over what was happening to Mitzi continued to nag at her.

Was Robert exacting his rage toward her onto Mitzi?

Griff hung up the phone and slanted her a worried look. "You okay?"

"I am, but Mitzi isn't." She paced in front of the fireplace. "I wonder what he's doing to her. If he'll keep her alive or—"

Griff stroked her back. "Don't go there, Ginny. I know you're terrified and I'm afraid for Mitzi, too. But Jacob and Liam will find her." He exhaled sharply. "Jacob is calling in emergency teams of deputies to search Whistler and its outskirts and Liam is on it. They'll pass the info on to Fletch so he can check places on the AT where Robert might hole up. We'll find him."

"What if we're not in time?" Panic made it difficult to breathe.

"Think positive," he said.

"You don't know Robert like I do." Ginny shivered. "He's cold and calculating. He gets pleasure out of inflicting pain."

"I'm beginning to realize just how depraved he is," Griff said in a voice tinged with disgust. "And I want to see him pay for what he did to you and Joy and every other woman he hurt."

"We need to do something. Robert has been playing games with me because he knew my weaknesses. I have to find out his and turn the tables on him."

Griff's brows shot up. "That's a good idea. What do you know about him?"

She searched her memory banks, filtering through the facade he'd presented and the few details he'd accidentally revealed. Were any of them true?

"Not much," she admitted. "Except that he lost his mother when he was young."

"Did he say what happened to her?"

She shook her head. "He refused to talk about it. Just said that she was gone and that his father raised him alone. He taught him everything he knew." A shudder coursed through her, but she stiffened her spine. "I thought he was referring to business, but what if he meant other things?"

"Like how he treated women," Griff filled in. "Oftentimes abused children become abusers."

"True," Ginny said. "The counselor I worked with after I escaped Robert gave me a ton of material to help me understand how an abuser chooses his victims. Predators are experts at reading others' weaknesses to use against them."

"He's violent and lacks self-control," Griff said. "What if he saw his father behave aggressively with his mother or with another woman?" Griff hesitated. "And the fire. Maybe…"

"Maybe what?"

"Perhaps his father liked to set fires, too," Griff said. "Or Robert could have been infatuated with fires

as a child. If so, there might be a record of him starting fires as a child or as a juvenile."

He snagged his phone again. "I'll call Liam and
suggest that he investigate that angle."

Ginny said a silent prayer they'd find something to
use against him.

MITZI WAS SWEET. And so pretty. He'd watched her ever
since he'd come to this hole-in-the-wall town.

But she wasn't Reese.

Sometimes he hated Reese. Wished he'd never met
her. That she hadn't seduced him and made him love
her. Made him want her so badly that he couldn't look
at another woman without comparing her to his beloved.

Joy certainly hadn't measured up. Sure, she'd accepted his advances. Had let him crawl into her bed.
She'd enjoyed his gifts and attention. But there had
been a desperation about her that disgusted him. As
if she knew she wasn't beautiful or smart enough. Her
body was full of imperfections. Her face a little too
made up and fake just like her personality.

She'd liked his money. He'd noticed that right away.

In the beginning, Reese had been impressed with
his gifts, too. But after a couple of months, she'd said
she didn't want them. Didn't want the fancy dinners or
dresses he chose for her. She'd even given him back the
diamond necklace and the blood-red ruby ring. When
he'd offered to sweep her away to Europe for a romantic getaway for a month, she'd balked and declared
she didn't want to be away from her sister that long.

Laughter bubbled in his throat. He'd fixed that, now hadn't he?

Mitzi looked up at him with wide, tear-stained eyes. Her sob caught in the gag he'd stuffed in her mouth. Her body shook with fear.

He sat down beside her where she lay tied on the bed and stroked her hair away from her face. The strands were damp from tears. And there was the missing chunk where he'd cut off a piece to send to Reese.

It wouldn't matter if her hair was long and pretty and perfect though. Not where she was going.

Chapter Eighteen

Ginny paced in front of the fireplace while Griff texted Liam about more information on Robert Bouldercrest.

As he hung up, he rolled his shoulders to alleviate his tension. He still reeked of smoke and soot from working the fire at Mitzi's Café.

The clock read four in the morning.

"Why don't you try to rest," he told Ginny. "Jacob has people searching for Mitzi. There's nothing else we can do until we get a lead or find more information on Bouldercrest."

"Maybe I could make a plea on the news, offer to exchange myself in return for Mitzi's safety," Ginny said with an urgency to her voice that made panic zing through him.

He shook his head, vying for calm when he wanted to shout, "Hell no."

"That's not going to happen, Ginny. Even if we set up a meet and exchange, you can't trust that he won't kill her."

Her face turned ashen, making him regret his harsh words. But he couldn't retract them because they were true. He certainly didn't intend to let Ginny offer herself up like some sacrificial lamb. Too many things could go wrong.

"I just feel so helpless," she cried. "Mitzi's with that maniac because of me and I'm just sitting here doing nothing."

Emotions overcame her and she sank onto the couch again and dropped her face into her hands. Her body trembled.

Unable to help himself, he crossed the room to her, sat down beside her and pulled her into his arms. "I know it's terrifying, but you're not alone now." He rubbed slow circles across her back, and she leaned into him and pressed her hand against his chest.

She was so small and delicate that he dropped a kiss against her hair and whispered soft assurances that everything would work out. She nestled against him and he closed his arms around her, praying he could deliver on his promises.

The warmth of the fire seemed to cocoon them into a more relaxed state, the sound of the crackling wood in the fireplace comforting. Her erratic breathing finally steadied, and she lifted her head and looked into his eyes. Griff's breath lodged in his throat.

In spite of the fear pounding in his chest, fear that mirrored hers, tension simmered between them. The kind of tension that stirred his desires and made him itch to be closer to her.

She placed her hand against his cheek, and he angled his head and studied her. The last thing he wanted to do was to frighten her or make demands upon her.

The tiniest inkling of sexual awareness flickered in her eyes, then they filled with longing and encouragement, and she parted her lips. He slowly leaned toward her. She leaned in at the same time, but he still hovered within an inch of her lips, determined to give her every opportunity to pull away if she wanted.

But she didn't pull away.

She tilted her head and pressed her lips to his. The kiss was gentle and so tentative that emotions he'd never experienced for another woman blossomed in his chest.

A second later, she threaded her fingers in his hair, drawing him nearer as she deepened the kiss. It took every ounce of his willpower not to lower her onto the sofa, climb on top of her and run his hands all over her sweet, supple body.

But this was Ginny, a woman who'd been bullied and abused and threatened. A woman who didn't readily trust.

He could not break the tentative bond he'd built, or the connection simmering between them.

Even if he couldn't have her, he'd protect her so that madman couldn't get to her.

GINNY HAD NO idea what had come over her, but every cell in her body screamed to kiss Griff. To let him hold her and chase away her demons, at least for a little while.

It had been so long since she'd kissed a man, or even wanted to kiss a man, that his lips sent a flurry of excitement and desire through her. Reservations whispered through her mind, but she ignored them.

Griff was nothing like Robert. He wasn't pushy or rough, hadn't tried to charm her pants off her. He'd done nothing except be honorable and protect her. Even now, in his arms, although strength and power emanated from his muscular body, his touch was tender and gentle.

She had no doubt that if she wanted him to stop, he would.

She just didn't want him to. Not yet anyway.

She craved the comfort of his arms and lips. Wanted to remember that once there had been joy in life, not just the mind-numbing fear, anger, grief and sadness consuming her for three years.

Griff stroked her back, their bodies rubbing together as he teased her lips apart with his tongue. She welcomed his sensual foreplay as the kiss became more frenetic. Hunger built inside her, heat and need making her cling to him, and she silently urged him to continue. He pulled away and looked into her eyes, questions lingering.

Affection for the handsome, sexy firefighter replaced the cautionary voice in her head, and she dragged his mouth back to her, taking what she wanted. His hands slowly roamed downward to her waist, and she ran her hands over his shoulders and back, reveling in the way his corded muscles flexed beneath her touch.

The sense that she had control emboldened her. She had the power to turn him on. To take without fearing he would force himself on her or explode violently if she decided to leave.

The realization was mind-blowing and cathartic and intensified her desire and her admiration for him.

As if he understood her needs, he trailed kisses

down her jaw and neck, suckling the sensitive skin of her throat as his hand moved toward her breast.

She arched into him, her breath puffing out in tiny pants that burst into the stillness of the night. The sound of the wind battering the glass broke into that stillness though and shattered the fog of desire wrapping its tentacles around her heart.

Griff seemed to understand that, too. He traced a thumb over her cheek, then cupped her face in his hands and kissed her again. This time there was hunger, but also the tenderness of a man's understanding and respect.

He gently pulled away from her, his breathing erratic. "I smell like smoke. I'm going to shower. Lie down and try to sleep, Ginny." He pressed a kiss to her forehead. "I'll be here, and the alarm is armed. Hopefully, tomorrow Liam and Jacob will have answers."

He was right. She couldn't allow herself to fall into bed with him and forget that it was her ex-lover who'd kidnapped Mitzi. That Mitzi's life was in his cruel hands.

She had to focus on the reason she'd come to Whistler. And falling for Griff Maverick had no part in it.

GRIFF DOVE INTO the shower, anxious to cleanse himself of the acrid scent of smoke and soot. Granted, he was accustomed to the odor, but when he'd kissed Ginny, he'd realized he'd wanted to come to her fresh and clean, not covered in the remnants of sweat and ash from his job. Or the violence created by her stalker.

The cool water helped alleviate his hard-on, then he cranked the temperature up to a blasting hot to scrub his body and hair. Smoke tended to linger and cling to every possible surface of his skin. He didn't want Ginny to associate the odor with him.

Forget it, man. She only kissed you out of gratitude. And fear. You're protecting her and she was afraid. That's it. Period.

Sobering at the thought, he soaped and scrubbed himself until his skin felt raw and every vestige of lust was wiped from his mind. Yet as he climbed out, dried off and pulled on clean sweats, a more disturbing thought hit him.

It wasn't just lust with Ginny. He was falling for her.

Except Ginny wasn't even her real name.

He had to remember that. When Bouldercrest was caught and put away, she would return to her life. She sure as hell didn't need another man attaching himself to her. Dreaming up unrealistic expectations. Trying to tie her down.

She needed her space. And to feel safe.

He'd damn well give that to her.

He towel-dried his hair, brushed his teeth, then went to check on her. She'd curled up on his couch and fallen asleep in front of the fire. Only she was tossing and turning, murmuring protests as if she was running from that madman in her sleep.

Exhausted and hating to see her suffer, he slid onto the sofa, lay down beside her and wrapped his arms around her. She snuggled into his arms, and he rubbed her back and dropped kisses into her hair, soothing her nightmares until she settled into a deep sleep.

He closed his eyes and held her, forcing his fears

about Mitzi at bay. He trusted Jacob and Liam to do their jobs. Tonight, he'd protect Ginny and get some rest.

He had to be prepared to help tomorrow if they got a lead on Bouldercrest. Or if Ginny decided to run again.

Exhaustion overcame him, and he drifted to sleep. But just like when he was on duty, he never truly relaxed. If the alarm sounded, he had to be quick on his feet.

Sometime later, sunlight crept through the curtains, jarring him to wake. He glanced at the clock. Seven thirty in the morning. He'd slept over two hours. Not bad considering the situation, he guessed.

Ginny sighed in her sleep, and he stroked her hair gently from her face. Lying on her side in his arms, she looked so peaceful that he didn't want to disturb her, so he hugged her tighter and lay there with her for another hour, listening to the wind blowing outside and the sound of birds chirping their morning song. Firelight flickered off her skin, making it look almost golden. Although the sight of the bruise on her cheek brought reality back with a vengeance.

"I'll take care of you," he whispered, willing his heart to be rational when it was already too late. Why had Ginny broken through the barrier around his heart now?

Especially when he and his brothers still needed to find his father's killer.

His phone buzzed on the coffee table. He stretched enough to snag it and checked the message.

Liam. Have information on Bouldercrest. Meet me in an hour?

Ginny shifted against him, and he struggled for control as her hips rubbed against his sex.

"Griff?"

Jacob's voice jerked him from his lustful thoughts.

He texted his brother in return. Stop by here. Don't want to leave Ginny alone.

A second passed. Then two. Liam responded that he'd be there in half an hour.

Griff eased himself from Ginny and laid her head on one of his throw pillows, then grabbed the afghan from the couch and draped it over her sweet body. Then he shuffled over to the kitchen and started a pot of coffee to brew while he hurried to take another shower.

A cold one to kill his morning erection before his brother arrived and started asking questions.

THE DELICIOUS AROMA of coffee brought Ginny out of a deep, exhausted sleep. She blinked to orient herself, then realized she was asleep on Griff's couch. The memory of his arms around her all night and his warm body pressed against hers taunted her.

She wanted to burrow into that place where she felt safe and…cared for.

Something she'd never felt with Robert. She had been a possession to him, someone to fill his needs. Hers hadn't mattered.

Footsteps from the kitchen brought her to a sitting position, and she saw Griff's back as he poured coffee into a mug. Firelight played off his broad shoulders and dark hair making him look sexy and tempting.

She had no business thinking about Griff and sex. "Coffee smells great," she said softly.

He turned to her with a small smile, then gestured to the mug. "Cream? Sugar?"

"Just black," she said. "I need something strong this morning."

"Me, too." He poured a second mug, then walked over to join her. He offered her a cup, and she took it, warming her hands with the hot mug.

"Liam is going to stop by in a few minutes. He has information on Bouldercrest."

Her pulse jumped. "Any word on Mitzi?"

"Not yet. I texted Jacob, and he said they're still combing the town and woods."

Ginny sipped her coffee. Every hour that passed dimmed the chances they'd find Mitzi alive.

"I'd better freshen up then." Suddenly self-conscious wearing the sweats Griff had given her to sleep in, she stood and carried her coffee with her to the guest bathroom. She closed the door, then studied herself in the mirror.

Hair tousled, eyes a little foggy from sleep, pale skin. What did Griff see when he looked at her?

A woman in trouble. One he was helping. *That's all.*

She splashed water on her face, then finger combed the tangles from her hair. Her color was starting to fade, her auburn roots showing through. Time for another dye job.

She needed another shower, too, but that could wait. Getting naked in Griff's bathroom with him and his brother nearby seemed too intimate. After they talked, she'd go to the inn, shower and change clothes. She needed a little distance between her and the handsome firefighter who made her suddenly want things she could never have.

She quickly dressed in the clothes she'd worn the day before, smoothed out the wrinkles on her shirt, then sipped her coffee as she returned to the den. Griff set a plate of cinnamon rolls on the coffee table.

"You made these?" she asked, impressed.

He chuckled. "They're from a can."

She laughed, which sounded foreign to her own ears.

The doorbell rang interrupting the moment, and he hurried to answer it while she refilled her coffee. His brother Liam appeared, solemn faced as he entered. Griff offered him coffee, and the men filled mugs then joined her in the den.

Liam spoke to her, then set a file on the table.

"Any word on Mitzi?" Ginny asked.

"Jacob thinks they found a cabin where Bouldercrest might have been staying, but he's gone. No sign of Mitzi at the moment, but Griff called in the SAR's dogs to track the scent."

Griff retrieved the baggie holding the river rock and Mitzi's hair and handed it to his brother. "This came last night. Somehow he found out Ginny was here."

Liam cursed beneath his breath, then reached for the file. "Let me tell you what I learned about Bouldercrest."

Ginny tightened her fingers around the mug as he opened the folder. "It took some digging, but I think this is the man you called Robert." He showed her a photograph, and Ginny confirmed that the image belonged to Robert.

"His real name is Ansel Holmes," Liam said. "His parents were Louise and Jimmy." Liam laid out a photograph of the remains of a burned house and then a picture of a small auburn-haired woman. "This is the mother. When Ansel was five years old, she died."

Ginny pressed her fingers to her mouth to stifle a gasp. His mother's hair was auburn…

"What happened?" Griff asked.

"Apparently the couple had marital issues," Liam filled in. "Neighbors reported domestic violence and police visited the house twice. According to a neighbor, the mother planned to leave her husband and take her son with her."

"But the father wouldn't let that happen," Ginny murmured.

"Right," Liam said. "Neighbor overheard Holmes tell his wife she'd never leave, and she certainly wouldn't take his son."

Ginny set her coffee on the table and twisted her hand in her lap. The conversation sounded too familiar.

"Then what happened?" Griff prodded.

"One night about a week after that incident, neighbors reported a fire at the house. When police arrived, they found the mother's body inside."

"Let me guess," Ginny said. "She was strangled?"

Griff cleared his throat. "And police speculated the fire was set to cover evidence?"

"Right again. But it gets even more disturbing," Liam said. "Police believe the son witnessed the murder."

A tense second passed. "Did they arrest the father?" Griff asked.

Liam shook his head. "He disappeared with the boy. That's when they became the Bouldercrest family."

"He learned to kill from his father," Ginny said under her breath. "And when I tried to leave him, it triggered the memory of his mother trying to leave." Because she had auburn hair.

And now in his mind, he was killing his mother over and over and over…

Chapter Nineteen

Ginny fought the urge to feel sorry for Robert. Witnessing his mother's abuse and murder had obviously traumatized him.

Yet not all kids from abused homes grew up to be killers.

"A profiler would say that he chose his victims as surrogates for the mother who he perceived abandoned him," Liam said. "It doesn't excuse his crimes, but understanding his thought processes can be helpful in finding him and eliciting a confession from him when we do."

"He doesn't think he did anything wrong," Ginny said matter-of-factly. "He functions on learned behavior and values. His father probably pounded it into his head that the man was head of the household, that the woman was subservient and supposed to obey."

"Archaic," Griff muttered.

His comment warmed Ginny's heart. Yet she was piecing together the dark corners of Robert's mental processes. "In his mind, he justifies his actions by how he was raised. He thinks he was good to me, to the other women, and that we were ungrateful for all he did for us."

"He's psychotic," Griff muttered.

"Narcissistic personality disorder," Liam said. "Combined with obsessive-compulsive disorder and the abuse. His father may have forced him to watch when he beat his mother, said he was teaching her a lesson and teaching him to be a good son."

"She was supposed to be the perfect wife," Ginny murmured. "I heard that more than once. Only I didn't measure up."

Griff squeezed her arm. "You do realize that it had nothing to do with you. That you weren't inadequate, Ginny. That none of this is your fault."

Her counselor had drilled the same sentiment over and over into her head. "I do. But when it's beaten into your skull, it's difficult not to feel that you did something wrong."

"Well, you didn't," Griff said. "Look at his past. His thinking is totally screwed up."

"Griff is right," Liam agreed. "With this type of disorder, nothing a woman or anyone else does can measure up to his twisted and unrealistic standards and beliefs."

"When someone really cares about you, they focus on the positive," Griff pointed out. "And on pleasing you. Not on what you can do for them or how they make you look."

Ginny sucked in a sharp breath. Griff was so much healthier mentally than Robert had ever been.

She tapped her foot on the floor. "So, what do we do now?"

"Our teams are looking for Mitzi, and my people are working to identify his aliases and locate him." Liam said. "Now that we have a profile and his picture, I'm going to release it to the media. Maybe someone in or around Whistler spotted him or has information about where he's staying."

"And where he took Mitzi," Ginny said.

"That, too."

"Let me make a personal statement on the news," Ginny offered.

Griff cleared his throat. "I told you no, Ginny."

She turned to Liam. "Please. Maybe I can reach him. After all, I'm the one he really wants."

Liam pulled a hand down his chin. "That's too dangerous. Give us a little time. If we don't find him, we'll consider setting that up."

She gritted her teeth. She appreciated the fact that he and Griff wanted to protect her. But what about what she wanted?

She was tired of men making decisions for her. If Mitzi died, she had to live with her death on her conscience, not them.

She'd driven to Whistler to find Robert. She would come up with her own plan and end this nightmare for good.

GRIFF WATCHED GINNY pace again as he stepped aside to talk to his brothers. "How do you think this information will help us find Bouldercrest?"

Liam shrugged. "It might not. But when we do locate him, we can use it to establish a personal connection. That connection could enable us to convince him to release Mitzi."

Griff hissed. *If* she was still alive. They had no idea.

"What can I do to help?" he asked.

"Ginny seems to trust you. Stay with her and make sure she doesn't do something stupid like go after Bouldercrest herself."

Griff wanted to argue that Ginny was smarter than that. And she was smart. But emotions could make a person do irrational things. And at the moment she was running on fear.

"We'll keep you posted if we hear something or find Mitzi."

Griff nodded and glanced back at Ginny as he closed the door behind his brothers. Her agitation was like a live force in the room.

She halted her frantic pacing with a sigh. "I need to go back to the inn and shower and change clothes."

"I'll follow you and we'll pick up your bags and bring them back here."

Her lips pressed into a frown. "All right."

He slipped on his jacket and retrieved his keys, turned off the gas logs and escorted Ginny outside.

The rain had passed although dark clouds still hovered, casting a grayness across the mountain. Trees swayed and the wind battered the bushes. The chill in the air hinted at another storm, maybe a tornado on its way.

Knowing Bouldercrest had been at his house, on his property, roused his anger. He scanned the yard and beyond for signs the maniac had returned. Maybe he hoped Griff would leave Ginny alone.

Not going to happen.

Traffic was minimal, but he kept his eyes peeled for trouble as he maneuvered the switchbacks on the winding mountain road back toward town. Ginny was right behind him in her car. When he pulled up to the inn, he noticed the deputy Jacob had assigned to stand guard for Robert at the inn parked in the drive in an unmarked car.

He threw up a hand in acknowledgement to the deputy, climbed out and walked Ginny up to the inn.

"You can go now," she told him when they stood on the porch.

"I'm not leaving," he said. "I'll walk you to the room then wait downstairs while you shower and gather your things."

She didn't look happy about it, but she didn't argue. They walked up the stairs together, and she unlocked the door. He placed his hand on her arm and insisted he enter first and check the room.

At first glance, everything appeared to be just as they'd left it. He took a quick sweep of the bathroom and didn't see anything troubling inside, so returned to the door.

Ginny walked over to her suitcase and unzipped the bag.

His phone buzzed on his hip. Jacob. He punched Connect.

"Griff, there's another fire. This time behind your house."

Dammit to hell.

"I'll send my deputy inside to stand watch over Ginny while you go home."

"What's wrong?" Ginny asked as he hung up.

"A fire behind my house. Jacob's there. I have to go." He explained about the deputy. "Stay inside your room, Ginny. Bouldercrest could have set this fire to lure me away from you, so don't go anywhere until I come back."

He gave her a quick hug, hurried out the door, waited until she locked it then jogged down the stairs.

IT WAS ALREADY HAPPENING. Robert was targeting Griff because he was helping her. No one was safe if they got close to her.

Why had she let down her guard for even a moment?

Praying Griff's house was okay and grateful his brother was meeting him there, she locked the door, then stepped into the shower. That kiss with Griff taunted her. Sweet and tender, but she'd tasted need and desire, a potent combination.

Griff knew how to respect a woman. To give, not simply take as Robert had done. To step away if she asked.

She didn't want to ask. She wanted him to kiss her again. To feel his lips on her and his arms around her and to know that she wasn't alone.

The hot water usually calmed her, but anxiety felt like needles pricking her skin. She quickly rinsed off, then towel-dried her hair and hurried to dress.

Just as she opened her suitcase, the sound of a telephone ringing echoed. She reached for her purse, then realized it wasn't her phone. A chill slithered through her as she felt in her bag. Buried beneath her underwear, she found a burner cell phone ringing.

Her heart raced, but she steeled herself as she answered. "Hello."

"It's good to hear your voice, love," Robert murmured. "I've missed you."

She closed her eyes and envisioned her sister's face in her mind. Felt her sister's terror as Robert had wrapped his hands around her throat.

Then Joy's face. She hadn't known the woman, but she imagined her shock and terror when she'd realized the man she thought charming was a sadistic animal.

And Mitzi, the sweet, friendly young woman who liked to bake.

"You took Mitzi, didn't you?"

"I warned you not to leave me."

"She has nothing to do with us, Robert. Please let her go."

"I can't do that now, love. You have to be taught a lesson."

Emotions thickened Ginny's throat. "I've learned my lesson. Just let her go."

His heavy breathing echoed over the line. "Not until you admit you belong to me. I told you that the first time we made love."

She swallowed hard at the memory. That night had started off tender and romantic. But when he'd held her arms above her head, looked into her eyes and declared that she was his, fear had rippled through her. The romance and tenderness had evaporated. In its place, she'd seen a dark, obsessive streak.

"I don't belong to you," she said matter-of-factly.

"I told you that when I left. But Mitzi shouldn't have to suffer because of me."

"And I told you that I'd never let you go."

His sinister tone made bile rise to her throat. "You killed Joy Norris, didn't you?"

A bitter laugh rumbled over the line. "She wasn't you, my love. No one else can ever take your place. Don't you know that by now?"

She inhaled slowly. "You need psychiatric help, Robert. Turn yourself in and get some counseling."

"There's nothing wrong with me, Reese. But when you make promises, you should keep them. And you promised yourself to me when you crawled in my bed."

He was twisting everything to his advantage. Her therapist had warned her that abusers were manipulative and made the victims feel as if they were at fault.

"I didn't promise to let you abuse me or murder anyone," she retorted. "Now let Mitzi go, Robert, and leave me alone."

"I will never leave you," he whispered darkly. *"Never."*

"But I don't love you." How could she love a monster?

"Because of that fireman," he said, his voice terse.

She breathed in and out again. "He has nothing to do with this."

"You spent the night with him," Robert said. "You cheated on me."

"We would have to be a couple for me to cheat on you," she quipped. "And we're not a couple and never will be."

A tense heartbeat passed. His breathing became

more erratic. "But we will be together again. And this time it will be forever."

"That's not going to happen, Robert. Forcing me and killing my sister and other women won't make me love you."

"Because you're in love with *him*?" he said bitterly.

No, she wasn't. Was she?

"Once he's gone, you'll come back to me."

She opened her mouth to tell him that Griff meant nothing to her. She had to protect him. But the line went dead in her hands.

GRIFF HIT THE ground running as soon as he made it back to his cabin. Relief hit him when he realized the fire hadn't spread to his house.

But he spotted the blaze in the woods behind his property, ran around the cabin to the backyard and down the hill into the brush. The fire engine had managed to park in close proximity to the burning leaves and trees, and his team was already geared up and spraying the flames from the fire hoses. Smoke billowed above the treetops and floated into the sky, a thick gray that obscured the clouds above.

Jacob stood at the edge of the scene, a grim look on his face. "Those boys didn't start this," he said as Griff joined him. "I've already checked with their parents and they're at home. Seems the parents took action after the interrogations and are monitoring their movements."

"It's Bouldercrest," Griff said, his pulse hammering. "He was here before. Now he's leaving me a message." That lighter he'd found at the ridge probably belonged to him. And so did the boot print.

Jacob wiped sweat from his brow. Already the scent of burned lumber and grass permeated the air, and ashes swirled in the breeze, the fire threatening to spread to other areas of the woods as the embers fell onto dry land.

"Griff, this man is extremely dangerous. Now that he knows Ginny stayed here with you, he's gunning for you, brother."

Griff gritted his teeth. "Don't worry about me, Jacob. I can take care of myself." But Ginny…she was vulnerable.

"Let me help my squad, then I need to get back to her."

Jacob gave him a worried look, but his phone buzzed, and he answered it while Griff jogged over to the fire truck, geared up and joined his team. The wind howled off the mountain, causing the flames to spread from one tree to another and feeding the fire.

"We've set up a perimeter," Baxter said as Griff took over one of the hoses. "Hopefully we can keep it contained."

"Any sign of point of origin?" Griff asked.

Baxter pointed toward the edge of Griff's property where a gas can lay in the bushes. "You got lucky. If the wind had been blowing uphill, it might have spread to your deck."

Lucky? Maybe. So far, he was alive, and his house had been spared. But what else did Robert Boulder-crest have planned?

He and his squad worked for the next hour to get the

blaze under control. By the time it had settled down and died out, he was sweating, angry and worried sick about Ginny.

Jacob had left with the gas can to send to the lab for prints. One of his team was assigned to stay and monitor conditions in case the wind sparked the embers and resurrected the fire.

He removed his gear and stowed it, then headed back to the inn. He called Ginny's cell phone on the way, but she didn't answer. He told himself she might be in the shower, but anxiety tightened every cell in his body.

By the time he arrived, he was in a state of near panic. He pulled into the drive and glanced at the unmarked car where the deputy was surveilling the inn.

His pulse jumped as he hurried to talk to the deputy. At first glance it appeared the man was sleeping on the job. His head was tilted to the side, and his body looked slumped.

Anger zinged through him. How could he sleep when he was supposed to be watching out for Ginny? What if something had happened?

He tapped the glass, but the man didn't respond. He tried again, but nothing. Heart hammering, he yanked open the door, and touched the deputy's shoulder.

When he still didn't move, Griff leaned inside, and tilted the man's head sideways. Dammit.

Blood. On the deputy's shirt. Chest. Hands.

He'd been shot in the chest. And he was dead.

MITZI LOOKED UP at him with frightened, doe-like eyes. She was a pretty girl.

Just not Reese.

"You just won't do," he murmured as he stroked her hair from her tear-stained cheek.

She wiggled and squirmed, twisted her hands to try to break the ropes binding them together.

Watching her fight made his body harden. He did like a fighter. As long as she learned her lesson and then accepted her proper place.

But her hair was wrong. Not the right color.

He pressed a kiss on her forehead, and she went bone still, tensing as if she might let him have his way if he'd release her.

Silly woman. He'd told her she wasn't right. Even if he took her or she gave herself to him and said she loved him, she still wouldn't be.

He gripped her face in his hands and squeezed her cheeks so tightly her eyes bulged. "It's up to Reese now if you live or die," he whispered. The same for the fireman. "It's all up to my Reese."

Chapter Twenty

Ginny imagined Griff's beautiful house being destroyed by fire, a house he'd practically built with his own hands, and nausea clogged her throat.

He'd lost his father in a fire, and now he was working to save his own house. What if Robert had started the fire and was there now? He could have set a trap for Griff.

She snatched her phone to call and warn him, but hesitated. She grabbed the burner phone but couldn't remember his number. Panic setting in, she considered calling the sheriff's office, but Jacob was at Griff's so he would protect him.

At least she hoped he did, she thought as she paced the room. She could not allow Robert to hurt Griff or Mitzi or anyone else.

She'd promised Griff she'd stay inside the room, but how could she sit here and do nothing when Robert might be mapping out his attack?

A plan began to form in her mind. She had to take charge. Stop him herself.

Nerves tightened her shoulders as she retrieved her gun, pulled on her jacket and stowed the weapon in her pocket. Then she called the number Robert had phoned from in the burner phone.

The phone rang once, then twice, then a third time. Finally, Robert answered.

"I've been expecting your call, love."

Her skin crawled. "Please don't hurt Mitzi or Griff," she said. "I'll do whatever you want. Just tell me where to come."

A long pause filled with his breathing. "Did he put you up to this?"

"He has no idea I've talked to you." She just hoped he was okay.

"How about the police? Are you working with the sheriff?"

"No," she said emphatically. "I'm alone. I just want this to stop. No one else has to get hurt, Robert."

His heavy breathing echoed over the line. "All right. I'll text you the address where to meet me. But it has to be tonight. And no calling the police or telling that damn fireman or Mitzi is dead."

Ginny's lungs strained for a breath. Now that she understood what made him tick, she'd play his game until she found Mitzi and confirmed she was safe. "I understand. I'll do whatever you say."

"You'd better, Reese. This is your last chance."

A knock pounded on the door, startling her. "Send me the address. And don't hurt Mitzi or the deal is off."

She didn't wait for a response. She ended the call herself.

"Ginny, are you in there? It's me, Griff!"

She threaded her fingers through her hair, then

rushed to the door and opened it. The sight of Griff's handsome face sent relief through her.

Robert hadn't managed to hurt him. At least not yet.

She intended to keep it that way. Which meant lying to Griff. Escaping from his watchful, protective eyes and facing Robert on her own.

"Thank God, you're all right." The strain on Griff's face eased a fraction, then he drew her into his arms. "I was afraid he'd hurt you."

"I'm okay." She curled her arms around him. "I was afraid he'd hurt you or burned down your house."

He eased away from her an inch, then brushed her cheek with his thumb. "My house is fine. But…"

"But what?"

"He killed the deputy watching the inn. I've already called Jacob."

Emotions flooded her. Sorrow. Guilt. Hatred for Robert.

And a deep fear for Mitzi and for Griff that cemented her decision to meet Robert alone.

GRIFF'S HEART WAS hammering so fast he thought his chest would explode. He soaked in the sight of Ginny's beautiful face riddled with panic and fear, and sadness twisted at his gut.

"Oh, God," she choked out. "Another man is dead because of me."

He regretted telling her, but he'd had no choice. She had to know the lengths Robert had gone to today. That it was imperative she stay with him so he could protect her.

"The deputy understood the dangers of the job, Ginny."

"That still doesn't make it right." Tremors rippled through her body, and he hugged her tighter.

"I know it's not right. He was a good man."

She gulped back tears. "Did he have family? Was he married? Did he have children?"

"No, no and no," Griff said. "He was divorced, had just moved here. I don't think he had family either, at least not that I know of."

A small cry broke from her, and he rubbed slow circles along her back. "Shh, it's all right."

"Nothing about this is all right."

"I know," he murmured. "But he did his job and we will find Robert. I promise."

"How many more people have to die before he's caught and locked away?" Ginny asked, bitterness darkening her tone.

"Hopefully no more." Griff pressed a kiss to her cheek. "I need to go back downstairs and wait on Jacob. I just had to make sure you were safe first." Although he'd left the body alone. That didn't sit well in his gut either. What if someone messed with the crime scene?

"What about the innkeeper?" Ginny asked.

"She's fine. The two guests who were registered checked out when they heard a policeman was stationed outside." He squeezed her arm. "Lock the door and stay in the room," Griff ordered.

Ginny shook her head. "I'll go with you."

"You don't need to see the deputy like that," Griff said. "I promise I'll return as soon as Jacob arrives."

A siren wailed from outside, and she pulled away from him. "All right. Go. I'll be here when you get back."

He hoped to hell she was, and that she didn't do anything stupid like try to leave without him.

GINNY LOCKED THE door as soon as Griff left the room. Then she walked over to the window, pushed the curtain aside and watched as Jacob climbed from his police car and hurried to the deputy's car.

Griff met them just as a hearse appeared and parked. It had to belong to the ME.

God, the day kept getting worse.

The men gathered around the deputy's car, but Griff's body blocked her view of the man inside. A van veered into the parking lot, and a team climbed out, wearing jackets with ERT on the back. They would work the crime scene and collect evidence.

Her stomach knotted as they snapped pictures of the car and deputy, then began to take ones of the surrounding ground and area. She hoped they gathered conclusive evidence, although if she found Robert first, they wouldn't need it.

She'd take care of him herself.

The thought made her feel sick inside, but she couldn't live with people dying on her account.

Tears for the deputy spilled from her eyes, and she brushed them away angrily. Griff spoke to his brother, then glanced up at the window, and their gazes locked.

He was the kind of tough, stubborn strong man who made a hero. She could so fall in love with him if things were different.

She might even learn to trust again.

He left Jacob and the ME and search team and walked toward the inn.

The phone Robert had left for her taunted her from the nightstand. Griff would want her to confide about the phone call.

But sharing with him would only endanger him. Tonight, she'd meet Robert and take care of him then everyone else would be safe.

The thought of dying didn't frighten her. Her life the past three years had not really been living. She didn't want to go to prison, but justice for her sister and all the others whose lives had been destroyed by Robert would be worth it.

A knock sounded at the door. "Ginny?"

She inhaled a calming breath, then turned the lock. Griff looked so handsome and sexy and worried that she wanted him more than she'd ever wanted anything in her life. Just one night with him.

Anything could go wrong when she met Robert. He might kill her. She might kill him and go to jail.

She didn't want to do either without the memory of one blissful night in Griff's arms.

Granted, she didn't deserve to be with him.

But she reached for him anyway. "Griff?" Her voice broke. It was full of need and desire.

He pulled her to him and kissed her with such longing and tenderness that she used her foot to shut the door, then tugged him toward the bed.

GRIFF HAD BEEN so pent up with fear and frustration that he desperately wanted to hold Ginny and feel that she was alive in his arms. Her sweet lips moving against his triggered desires that heated his blood and nearly shattered his self-control.

No, he could control himself. If she wanted, he'd stop.

She teased his lips with her tongue, probing, searching, asking for more. Erotic sensations shot through him, stirring hunger and passion.

But the reminder of the dead deputy outside and how Ginny had suffered barreled through his brain at full speed, and he slowly ended the kiss and pulled away so he could look into her eyes.

"Ginny, I can't do this."

Her lips parted. Her breath panted out. "Why not? You don't want me?"

God, she was killing him.

"I do," he murmured. "But I like and respect you too much to take advantage of you after the way you've suffered."

She threaded her fingers through his hair, then rose on her tiptoes and kissed him again. "You aren't taking advantage."

"But Robert—"

"You're nothing like him and I know it." She traced her fingers along his jaw. "Please, Griff. I want to be with you, to replace all those bad memories with sweet, tender ones. Give me that."

He studied her for a moment. Felt the beating of her heart as her chest rose and fell against his. No woman had ever touched his heart the way she had.

Or stirred his body to such deep desires.

"Ginny, are you sure?" he whispered.

Her lips tilted into a seductive smile, and she kissed

him again. This time he didn't hesitate. He scooped her into his arms, carried her to bed then lay down beside her.

She curled into his arms, wrapped her leg around his thigh and pressed her body against his. Pleasure burst inside him, and he kissed her again, then plunged his tongue into her mouth, loving her the way she'd asked.

GINNY RAKED HER hands across Griff's muscular back as he trailed kisses down her neck and throat. Her body tingled with erotic sensations, and she urged him closer, savoring the feel of his hard body over hers.

He moved his hand to her breast, and she moaned in pleasure, whispering his name in a plea for more. Her breath panting out, she lifted her fingers and pulled at his T-shirt. He raised his body enough to yank it over his head and toss it to the floor.

"I smell like smoke," he murmured. "I should shower."

"I don't care." She cupped his face in her hands. "I want you now, just like you are."

The sexy smile he gave her sent tingles through her, and she pulled at his belt buckle.

His breath rasped out. "If you want me to stop at any time, just say the word."

"I won't want you to stop," she murmured. She'd never been more sure of anything in her life.

He helped her remove his clothing, shedding it in seconds, then he slowly undressed her, teasing her skin with gentle fingers and lips as he peeled her garments away.

Finally, naked, he kissed her again, then lowered

his head and traced his tongue over her nipple. She moaned a little sigh of pleasure, then rubbed her hands over his back. His thick muscles bunched and flexed as he tugged her nipple into his mouth and suckled her. He loved one breast, then gave the other the same titillating treatment, and she wrapped her legs around him and stroked his calf with her foot.

He groaned, then moved lower and flicked his tongue down her body, teasing her with erotic kisses until he spread her legs and dipped his tongue inside her. Pure pleasure shot through her in such waves that her body began to quiver with sensations. He cupped her bottom in his hands and lifted her hips to give him better access, then drove her over the edge with his fingers and mouth until a million butterflies burst inside her, and she cried out with her orgasm.

She whispered his name, begging him for more, and he climbed above her and looked into her eyes.

"Ginny?"

"Please." She slid her hand to his hard, thick length and stroked him. Hunger and pleasure darkened his eyes, and he moaned her name. He rolled sideways and disappointment seized her. Was he was going to leave her?

Then he grabbed a condom from the pocket of his pants, ripped open the package and rolled it on.

She helped him, desire building again with the anticipation of having that hard length filling her. Seconds later, he stroked her inner thighs with his sex, then pushed her legs farther apart and probed her womanhood.

One touch, one stroke, and pleasure soared to life again. He thrust into her, then pulled out, then entered her again, teasing and pleasuring her and building a rhythm that soon turned frantic with raw hunger. Over and over again, he thrust deeper and deeper each time until they were both panting, and their orgasms came together.

Groaning, he lowered his head and kissed her again, deeply and intimately, as the waves of pleasure rocked through them.

Both sated and breathless, he rolled to her side and pulled her into his arms, then they fell asleep wrapped around each other.

Sometime later, Ginny woke to the sound of a small beep. Sunlight had faded and dusk was setting in, shadows filling the room. She glanced sideways and saw Griff's handsome, protective face and his strong jaw, relaxed in sleep.

Her heart thudded. God help her. She'd fallen in love with him.

The beep punctuated the air again. The burner phone.

She hated to leave the warmth and safety of Griff's arms, but Robert was calling. She could never have a life with Griff until Robert was out of her life permanently.

Not that she'd have one after she finished with Robert. But she had to finish…

Slowly, she extricated herself from Griff's arms. He must have been exhausted from the last few days of firefighting and taking care of her, because he moaned slightly but didn't wake. She slid from bed, grabbed the burner phone and checked the text.

Robert had sent an address, GPS coordinates.

Come alone or Mitzi dies.

Chapter Twenty-One

Ginny quickly dressed, stowed her gun in her jacket pocket, then snatched her purse and keys. Just as she was tiptoeing toward the door, Griff stirred from sleep.

He would try to stop her if he woke up. Thinking on her feet, she dropped her bag then hurried over and grabbed the end of the sheet that they'd kicked from the bed. She lowered herself onto the mattress, eased his arms above his head and slipped the sheet around his wrists and tied it high on the bedpost. Just as she was finishing securing the knots, he opened his eyes.

He looked startled for a moment, then surprised as if he thought she was playing some sex game. "What are you doing, Ginny?"

She hated to disappoint him, but better that than have him dead.

She tightened the knot, then dropped a kiss on his cheek. "I'm sorry, Griff. But I have to go."

His brows shot up in alarm. "What?"

She glanced at his naked body and wanted nothing more than to crawl back in his arms and make love to him again. Now that he'd awakened that part of her where she could feel again, it was hard to walk away from it.

But she couldn't stay with Griff. Robert was waiting. And if she didn't do as he said, he would kill Mitzi, then he'd come after Griff. She cared too much about him to let him endanger himself for her.

"I have to leave."

He raked his free hand through his hair. "You're not going anywhere. Robert could be waiting outside."

She squared her shoulders and stepped away from the bed. "He is waiting for me. And if I don't come to him, he's going to kill Mitzi."

Anger darkened his eyes. "Then we'll call Jacob. He'll track him—"

"No." She pulled the gun from her pocket. "He said to come alone, or he'd kill her."

"Ginny, please, listen to me. It's a trap, don't you see that?"

"Of course, I do. I'm not a fool. At least not anymore." She lifted the gun. "I'm going to play along then get him out of my life forever."

He jerked at the sheet and moved his legs to the side of the bed. "Untie me, Ginny. You can't face him alone. It's too dangerous."

"It's more dangerous if I don't do as he says." Her hand shook slightly as she trained the gun on his chest. "I'm not going to let Mitzi die because I'm afraid of Robert."

"Please, Ginny," Griff pleaded. "He'll probably kill her anyway, then kill you or abduct you and do God knows what."

Her anger rallied, swift and fast. "This ends tonight.

I have to do it for my sister and Mitzi and Joy and all the other women he hurt or will hurt in the future."

He jerked at the binding around his wrists, making the bed post rattle. "Please, let me go. I can hide in the car with you. He won't even know I'm there."

Tears pricked her eyes. He was so brave, and strong and caring. He risked his life every day for others.

Today was not the day he'd lose his life. At least not for her.

"Thank you for last night," she said in a pained whisper. Then she turned and walked out the door and hurried out to her car.

She plugged the GPS coordinates into her phone, drove from the parking lot and headed out of town to meet the man who'd destroyed her life. She refused to allow him to destroy anyone else's.

GRIFF BELLOWED GINNY'S name as the door closed behind her. He couldn't believe she'd made love to him and now was leaving him here while she faced that monster alone.

And what did she mean—she was going to end it? What did she have planned?

He jerked at the sheet, but the knot was fast and tight. Furious and afraid for her life, he rolled sideways and struggled to reach the top of the bed post where she'd secured the knot. The little vixen had made certain it was secure and tied it in several places along the post.

Perspiration trickled down his neck as he stretched his body upward on the headboard and twisted his hands so he could reach the top. He wiggled and worked the fabric, slowly easing it loose and managed to release the first knot.

On to the second. With every moment he worked, Ginny was getting closer and closer to Bouldercrest. Why hadn't she let him go with her?

She had a gun, but did she know how to use it? He'd seen her fight that day the man attacked her on the street, but Bouldercrest could take her by surprise and she might not be able to fend him off, or get a shot in.

And what if he took the gun from her and shot her with her own weapon?

His heart pounded so hard he could hear the blood roaring in his ears. The second knot finally slipped free.

It took him another fifteen minutes to release his wrists from the post. By then the images bombarding him made his blood pulse with fear. With sweaty palms, he snatched his phone, pressed Jacob's number and reached for his clothes. When Jacob answered, he was dragging on his pants.

"Jacob, listen, Ginny heard from that bastard and she's gone after him."

Jacob heaved a breath. "Are you with her?"

Self-disgust ate at him. He'd let his emotions cloud his judgment and had slept with her. Had she seduced him so she could tie him up and get away?

"Griff?"

"No. Long story, but she's gone, and she has a gun. He told her to come alone or he'd kill Mitzi."

Jacob spewed a litany of curse words. "Did she say where she was supposed to meet him?"

Griff yanked on his shirt, fumbling with the buttons. "No. She just took off."

"All right, I'll call Liam and see if we can trace her phone."

"I'll meet you at the station."

Jacob agreed, and Griff shoved his feet into his shoes, then snatched his jacket and ran for the door.

GINNY'S HEAD WAS spinning as she veered down the narrow, winding road leading to the area where Robert requested they meet. Giant trees and brush enveloped her into an eerie world where the tunnel through the forest felt endless and eerie.

Robert would choose a remote location, some place he thought no one would find him.

Or hear her if she screamed.

She bounced over a rut in the road, making her stomach lurch, and struggled to tamp down her fear. The sweet taste of revenge roused her courage, and she plunged on, weaving around twists and turns until she reached a clearing that ended on a ridge. A small cabin sat near the edge, rustic and weathered, and the yard was overgrown with weeds encroaching on the patchy grass.

Wind beat at the loose shutters, causing them to flap, and making the deserted place look cold and desolate. Aware Robert would be hiding out, watching her approach, she scanned the area in search of him as she braked to a stop. Her hand automatically flew to her gun, an image of her sister's face flashing behind her eyes.

"Today is for you, Tess."

Resignation and determination washed over her as she climbed from the car. She turned in a wide circle, hoping Robert would be a man and meet her face-to-face.

Instead, the sound of a woman screaming echoed in the wind.

Mitzi.

Her heart jumped to her throat, and she took off running toward the house. She'd come here to save Mitzi and she wouldn't back down now.

She crossed the grass and climbed the steps to the porch, her eyes trained for Robert. But he was nowhere in sight. Probably skulking in the shadows like a coward.

She twisted the doorknob, and it creaked open. The interior was dark and dank, and wind whistled through the eaves of the old boards of the house. One step in and the wooden floor squeaked. She paused to listen for Mitzi again. A noise sounded from a back room to the right.

Scuffling? Mitzi crying?

Her heart wrenched.

She slowly eased toward the hallway, her hand over her gun in her jacket pocket, ready to pull it when Robert appeared. Another step and Mitzi's cry grew louder. She passed a small room that appeared empty, then a bathroom that was dirty and hadn't seen paint in a decade or more. Then a second bedroom. Just as she was about to enter it, the floor creaked behind her.

Her fingers wrapped around the handle of her gun. Before she could pull it from her pocket Robert wrapped his arms around her neck in a choke hold and dragged her into the room.

BY THE TIME Griff met Jacob at the sheriff's office, Liam had a trace on Ginny's phone. Jacob peeled from the parking lot and sped through town, siren blaring.

Griff's stomach knotted every time he imagined what Robert might do to Ginny.

She was tough and strong and a survivor. She deserved to be treated with love and respect. He had the desperate urge to be the one who showed her how a man should love a woman.

How could he have fallen for her in such a short time?

Especially when she'd lied to him.

Had she simply used him the night before to distract him so she could confront Robert on her own?

He didn't want to believe she would do that. She'd been abused and stalked to the point he'd worried she wouldn't want a physical relationship. Yet she'd come apart in his arms.

The connection he'd felt with her had to be real, didn't it?

"How did she get away from you?" Jacob asked.

Humiliation shot through Griff. "She pulled a gun."

"Dammit. Why didn't she call me?" Jacob asked.

Griff remembered the fear haunting her eyes. And the guilt lacing her voice. "She's afraid," he said.

"All the more reason not to go off alone."

"I know, but this bastard murdered her sister and she blames herself. She believes it's her fault he killed Joy and kidnapped Mitzi."

Jacob pressed his lips into a thin line. "Guilt is pretty powerful, isn't it?"

Griff studied his brother's deep scowl. They'd never really talked about their father's death. "It wasn't your fault that Dad didn't survive the hospital fire," Griff said. "I'm the firefighter. I should have insisted he stay outside."

Jacob made a low sound in his throat. "Don't do that, Griff. It wasn't your fault either. Dad did what Dad did, his job. That scene was chaotic, and lives were at stake. We needed manpower. None of us could have just stood by and watched without helping."

Griff's throat felt thick with emotions. Jacob was right. He'd blamed himself, but the only way he could have stopped his father from running into the hospital to help save lives was to have knocked him unconscious.

The Maverick men were protectors. That instinct had been bred into their blood when they were born.

Jacob swerved onto a graveled road that appeared to lead nowhere, and he sped around the winding curves as he followed the GPS coordinates Liam had sent. The storm clouds disappeared beneath the thick overhanging trees, casting the road into such darkness that Jacob had to turn on his headlights.

Three miles down the winding road, they finally broke into a clearing. Griff's heart stuttered at the sight of Ginny's car.

"She's here," he said.

"Stay in the car and let me handle this," Jacob said. "He might be armed."

"No way." Griff reached for the door handle.

Jacob held up a warning hand. "Then stay behind me and follow my lead. The last thing I want is for you to get shot by a stray bullet if Ginny fires at Bouldercrest."

Griff nodded, then said a silent prayer that Ginny was all right as they eased their way toward the house.

THE SOUND OF crying roused Ginny from unconsciousness. Reality crashed back with the force of a tornado, infuriating her. Robert had gotten the best of her.

After all her training and armed with a weapon, he'd won.

She blinked and tried to focus on her vision. No... she refused to give up. She had to think.

She felt something along her arm, then her cheek and opened her eyes. Robert. He was stroking her face with his fingers.

Her skin crawled.

For a moment, she considered spitting in his face, but that would do nothing except incite his anger. She had to outsmart him.

Think, Ginny, think.

Mitzi's muffled cry echoed nearby, and she glanced sideways. The young woman was tied and gagged, curled on a cot in the corner, her hands secured to the bedpost.

She'd left Griff the same way. Except she'd done it to protect him, not hold him hostage.

"Robert," she murmured.

"I'm here, love. I told you we'd be together soon."

Emotions threatened to make her ill, but she swallowed back the bile. *Use what you know about him.*

Get inside his head. "I know why you were so upset when I left," she said softly. "I understand now."

His fingers stopped moving across her cheek. "What do you mean? You know?"

She feigned a smile. "Your father hit your mother, so she decided to leave him, didn't she? But he wanted her to stay."

Robert's jaw tightened, eyes flickering with a myriad of emotions.

"You watched him beat her, didn't you? He told you mothers and wives weren't supposed to leave. Then he killed her."

Razor-sharp anger blazed on his face. "They're not supposed to leave. They're supposed to be faithful and love you forever."

"That's the reason you tried so hard to hold on to me," she said in a low whisper. "I realize that now. Now that I understand, I think we can make it work."

His Adam's apple bobbed as he swallowed, his eyes shifting as if he was debating whether or not to believe her.

"We'll talk things through," she continued softly. "Everything will be different between us this time."

"How different?" he asked, his voice rough with emotions.

"We'll be together, and we'll talk. And I won't leave." She smiled at him again, although her stomach was heaving in protest. "Please untie me and I'll show you how much I've missed you."

He trailed his fingers over her throat, then around her breast, and she choked back a cry of revulsion.

"Please," she whispered. "I want to touch you and give you pleasure."

Desire sparked in his ugly gray eyes, and he slipped his fingers up and began to untie her while he kissed her neck and throat. Ginny closed her eyes and willed herself to play along, but hatred, deep and dark, bloomed like a cancer inside her.

Finally, he freed the last knot around her hands, then he held them above her head and crawled on top of her. Panic threatened. She had to reverse the situation.

She gripped his hands with her own, then flipped him over to his back. He looked startled, but she lowered her head and kissed his cheek to assuage his alarm. "I told you, I want to show you how much I missed you. Let me pleasure you first, then you can have your way with me just like you did when we first met."

Excitement and lust. A chuckle rumbled from him and he rubbed himself against her. "I like the new Reese. Maybe I'll start calling you Ginny, too."

She smiled, clenched his hands and straddled him.

"You wanna play rough?" he asked.

"Just like you like it." She held his hands tightly, pushed her knee between his legs then suddenly kicked upward with her knee and jabbed him in the groin. He bellowed in pain and grabbed at his sex.

"What the hell?"

Taking advantage of the moment, she spotted her gun on the table across the room then dove for it.

He recovered and grabbed at her leg, but she kicked at his face and scrambled away. He chased her, caught her arm and flung her against the wall. Her head snapped backward, and she tasted blood, but she called on the skills she'd learned in self-defense and swung her arm up to deflect his assault when he came at her.

A swift thrust into his belly, and he doubled over. She kicked him in the groin again, then raced for the gun.

Breath panting out, she closed her fingers around it, turned and aimed it at his chest as he bellowed his rage.

Chapter Twenty-Two

Griff heard noises from the rear of the house the minute he entered the front door. Jacob had circled around the side of the house to the back to scope out the situation.

But Griff forged on. If Bouldercrest was armed, he'd deal with it.

The floor creaked as he eased down the hallway toward the source of the noise. He'd heard sounds that indicated a fight. A woman's muffled sobbing. Then Bouldercrest bellowing in rage.

He couldn't afford to waste a minute.

He crept to the door and peered inside to assess the situation. Mitzi lay on a cot in the corner, tied and gagged. He visually swept the room and found Bouldercrest against the far wall, his hands up in surrender as Ginny pointed a gun at him.

Instead of looking afraid though, Bouldercrest looked excited. The crazed look in his eyes indicated he was planning his next move. Twice Ginny's size, he could take her down in a minute.

"You deserve to die, Robert," Ginny said. "You killed Tess, the only person in the world I loved."

"That was your fault," Bouldercrest barked. "I told you you'd be sorry if you left me."

"I was not your possession." Ginny's hand trembled, the gun bobbing up and down. "And I never will be."

"You're such a liar," Bouldercrest said. "A few minutes ago, you said you missed me and that you'd do whatever I said."

"I said I'd show you how much I missed you and I'm going to." She took a step closer to Bouldercrest and aimed the gun at the man's chest.

"You won't shoot me," the bastard said calmly. "You don't have what it takes to pull that trigger."

The damn fool was taunting her, practically challenging her. "You're wrong," Ginny said, her voice calm but filled with a deep-seated hatred. "You changed me, Robert. I'm not that sweet, meek person you first met."

Her finger moved to the trigger, and Griff's breath stalled in his chest. He stepped to the doorway. "Don't do it, Ginny," he murmured.

Footsteps echoed on the wood floor, and Griff knew Jacob was behind him. "Let me handle it," Jacob said in a low voice.

Griff threw up a warning hand. "I've got it, Jacob."

"Go away," Ginny told Griff and Jacob. "He deserves to die."

"That may be true," Griff said. "And maybe he changed you in some ways. He made you tougher and more wary of people. But don't let him turn you into a killer."

Ginny made a strangled sound. "He has to pay for what he did. I need justice for my sister and all the other lives he destroyed."

"He'll get justice," Griff said. "I promise. He'll go to prison for the rest of his life."

"But my sister is gone forever," Ginny cried.

Griff barely breathed out. "I know, and I'm sorry. I understand what it's like to lose someone you loved. You know I do."

A tear trickled down her cheek. "What about Joy? And the deputy? They died because of me."

"No, Ginny," Griff said. "They died because this man is a sadistic cold-blooded killer. But you're not. You have love and goodness in you."

Bouldercrest released a sarcastic laugh. "You don't know anything about me. Only a man who can't get his own woman tries to steal another man's."

"I'm not your woman," Ginny shouted. "Griff is ten times the man you are. Real men don't have to bully women into being with them."

Bouldercrest stepped toward her, his hands clenched as if he wanted to choke her, and Ginny pulled the trigger. Bouldercrest froze as the bullet pinged the floor beside his feet.

"Move again and you're dead," Ginny snapped.

Jacob cleared his throat. "Ginny, let me have the gun. I'll arrest him and haul him to jail myself."

Her eyes darted toward Griff and Jacob, but she shook her head. "I came here to get justice for Tess. And I won't leave without it."

"Then think about your sister," Griff murmured. "What kind of person was she? What would she want you to do? Would she want you to commit murder in her name?"

EMOTIONS CHOKED GINNY as Griff's words hacked at her thirst for revenge. Her sister loved people, animals, children. She was an artist and saw the world through hopeful eyes, through her love of nature and its wonders.

Would Tess want her to destroy her life for revenge? To live with anger and hatred?

Her hand wavered. She couldn't breathe. Her sister was gone, and all the beautiful colors died with her.

"I understand what it feels like to want revenge," Griff said. "For a while after my father died, I wanted the same thing. I thought if I found the person who'd set that fire, I'd beat the hell out of him. But then one day when I looked at his picture, I heard his voice talking to me. Telling me to respect women and children and to protect others. That day I realized if I sought revenge, it would eat away at my soul. And I would be desecrating his memory."

Ginny clamped her teeth over her bottom lip, her hand shaking.

"So, I decided to honor his memory by being the kind of man he'd want me to be." He inched closer to her. "I never met your sister, but I can't imagine she'd want you to throw away your life by going to prison for murder. Would she?"

Pain and grief twisted at Ginny. "No, she wouldn't."

"I think she'd want you to live your life and be happy. To show this bastard that he didn't break you."

"He has to be punished," Ginny said.

"Yes, he does." Griff took another step closer to her. "He deserves to rot in prison. To have to face the people he hurt and live with that every day."

Emotions tore at Ginny, pulling her in different directions. Griff was right. But could she let Robert live?

She'd wanted revenge for so long, she didn't know what to do with herself without it.

She heaved a wary breath. "How did you get past the anger?"

"I still get angry," Griff admitted. "But I have my brothers."

"That's just it," Ginny said in a pained whisper. "I have no one."

Griff placed a hand on her shoulder. "You're not alone, Ginny. You have me."

His soothing words helped heal her battered soul, and her rage dissipated. Griff was right. Her sister would want her to live her life for her.

She lowered the gun, but just as she did, Robert lunged toward her.

"Very touching, you tramp," he snarled.

Griff gripped Ginny's arm to pull her out of the way, then a gunshot sounded.

Jacob. Robert went down with a loud shout of pain, hugging his leg. Griff eased the gun from Ginny and covered Jacob while Jacob handcuffed Bouldercrest. Then he pulled Ginny into his arms.

When the bastard was secure, Jacob hurried to the cot where Mitzi lay, tied and gagged, her eyes wide in shock. He quickly untied her, then phoned for an ambulance.

Ginny pulled away from Griff, ran over to Mitzi and sank onto the bed beside her. "I'm so sorry, Mitzi. So sorry," Ginny whispered.

Mitzi was trembling, her cheeks red with tears, eyes swollen, her face pale. "He…was crazy."

"I know." She hugged Mitzi and held her, comforting her while they waited for the ambulance.

TWO HOURS LATER, after Mitzi was transported to the hospital, examined, and doctors reported that she was fine physically, she was released and sent home.

Bouldercrest underwent surgery to have the bullet removed from his leg and was moved to a prison facility with medical care to await his trial.

Jacob went home to his pregnant wife and stepdaughter, and Griff drove Ginny back to the inn. She'd been quiet and withdrawn ever since they left the hospital.

Griff walked her to her room and escorted her inside. "It's over now, Ginny," he murmured.

"I know. It's hard to believe. Thinking about what he did and wanting to catch him has consumed me for three years."

He feathered a strand of hair from her cheek. "Maybe you can start to heal now."

She looked up into his eyes, but instead of peace, turmoil still streaked her face.

"I meant what I said back there," Griff said. "You're not alone. I'm here for you."

Her eyes narrowed. "I…appreciate you saying that, Griff. But you don't have to protect me anymore."

His pulse jumped. "What if I want to be part of your life?"

A wave of sadness tinged her eyes. "I need time."

Emotions roughened his voice. "What are you going to do?"

"I don't know. That's what I need to figure out."

He offered her a tender smile. "I could help you do that."

She shook her head. "Thank you for everything you've done, Griff. But I need to be alone for a while." She rose on her tiptoes and kissed his cheek, then walked him to the door.

Griff left, his heart heavy. Why did he sense that Ginny had just said goodbye to him?

Chapter Twenty-Three

Two weeks later

Ginny laid a bundle of sunflowers on top of her sister's grave and sank down beside it.

"It's really over, Tess," she whispered. "Robert Bouldercrest is in prison and according to the police, he'll never be free again. They've charged him with four counts of murder, kidnapping, stalking and assault." The gas can and the lighter Griff had found had Robert's prints all over them. So did Ginny's room at the inn. Robert confessed to setting the wildfires as a diversion.

Jade had called to report that the man who'd attacked her in the alley was a drifter who'd been passing through. They'd caught him assaulting another woman and trying to steal her purse outside a hotel on the edge of town and he was in jail.

As the news sank in, Ginny—Reese—had finally begun to relax again and had taken back her real identity. Although she'd probably always look over her shoulder and she fully intended to keep up her self-defense training, she'd started sleeping better and the nightmares were fewer and further between.

She'd stowed her gun in a safe and hoped she never felt the need to pull it out again.

"I'm so sorry I let you down." Tears fell freely from her face, but she didn't bother to wipe them away. She pressed her hand over her mother's grave. "I'm sorry I didn't take care of her, Mother. I…wish I could turn back time. Be smarter."

Forgive herself. She was still struggling with that.

Suddenly sunshine burst through the dark storm clouds, and a rainbow streaked the sky, the colors dancing across her sister's grave.

Reese's breath stuttered. Then she looked down at the ground and saw flower buds beginning to push through the ground.

Flower buds in all different colors.

Emotions overcame her, and she pressed a kiss to her fingers then to Tess's tombstone.

Beloved Sister, Best Friend and Wonderful Artist.

Tess had brought so much life into the world, had loved and lived in the moment, had painted landscapes full of joy and beauty.

The rainbow, the flowers…was her sister trying to send her a message?

Looking up at the rainbow again, she felt a burst of hope for the future. She whispered that she'd be back, then hurried toward her car.

An hour later, she studied the mountains in the distance as she drove toward Whistler. She'd dreamed of Griff every night and wanted to talk to him again.

To see if a future for them might be possible.

The temperature warmed with each passing hour, and she noticed tiny flower buds on the trees dotting the mountainside.

Griff's words about honoring her sister by living her life were going to be her new mantra. Now that she'd decided what that path would be, she wanted to tell Griff about it.

Her car chugged around the winding mountain road, and she slowed as she approached Griff's cabin. It looked even more picturesque now with the wild-flowers blooming on the mountain and the sun slanting off the dark green foliage.

Nerves gathered in her belly as she parked, climbed out and walked up to the front door. What if Griff didn't feel the same way about her? What if he didn't love her?

She almost turned around but stopped herself. She'd overcome her worst fears by facing down the man who'd terrorized her. That had taken courage.

She had to summon her courage now. Still, her heart was on the line.

But instead of running away, she wanted to run toward her future. She only hoped Griff would be in it.

She'd started by changing her hair back to its natural color. No more colored contacts either. No more Ginny Bagwell.

Feeling more like herself, she rang the doorbell and twisted her hands together as she waited. A minute later, the door opened, and Griff stood on the other side, looking so sexy and handsome that her stomach fluttered. Surprise flickered in his eyes, then a smile, bolstering her courage.

"I missed you," she said, then mentally kicked herself. That wasn't how she'd planned to start the conversation.

His smile widened. "I missed you, too."

Relief whooshed through her, and she offered him her hand. "I have things to tell you, but first I want to introduce myself. My name is Reese Taggart."

His gaze met hers, and he nodded. "Hello, Reese." Then he cocked his head to the side. "You remind me of someone."

"I do?"

He nodded. "Yes, someone I fell in love with."

"That girl, the one who wanted revenge and lied to you…she's gone."

"I hope she's found peace," he murmured.

"She has. I mean I have."

A smile glittered in his dark eyes.

"As a matter of fact, I've decided to use my story to help others. I've been working on a series of articles about domestic violence." She licked her suddenly dry lips. "I'm also studying counseling so I can become a victim's advocate for domestic violence victims."

"Really?"

She tucked a strand of hair behind her ear. "I talked to your sister-in-law Jade about it when she called to update me on Robert's case."

"I think that's a great idea, Ginny—I mean, Reese."

"I just wanted to tell you." She hesitated a minute. Her courage faltered, and she started to leave.

"Wait," he said. "Don't go."

She looked into his eyes and felt a connection that rocked her back on her heels.

"I fell in love with Ginny," he said, "and that girl was part of you. I think I'm going to love Reese even more."

Then he pulled her into his arms, closed his mouth over hers and kissed her.

Six weeks later, she said *I Do* to the man she loved in the gazebo Griff built for their wedding behind the home they would share together.

As she kissed her husband, she heard her sister's angelic voice singing to her from the heavens.

* * * * *

Look for the final book in
USA TODAY *bestselling author*
Rita Herron's Badge of Honor miniseries
when Suspicious Circumstances
goes on sale next month!

And don't miss the previous titles
in the Badge of Honor series:

Mysterious Abduction
Left to Die

Available now wherever
Harlequin Intrigue books are sold!

#1953 SUSPICIOUS CIRCUMSTANCES
A Badge of Honor Mystery • by Rita Herron

Special agent Liam Maverick asks for nurse Peyton Weiss's help in his hunt for the person who caused the hospital fire that killed his father. But someone doesn't want Peyton to share what she knows...and they'll do whatever it takes to keep her quiet.

#1954 TEXAS KIDNAPPING
An O'Connor Family Mystery • by Barb Han

After stopping a would-be kidnapper from taking her newly adopted daughter, Renee Smith accepts US Marshal Cash O'Connor's offer of a safe haven at his Texas ranch. The case resembles his sister's unsolved kidnapping thirty years ago, and Cash won't allow history to repeat itself.

#1955 THE LINE OF DUTY
Blackhawk Security • by Nichole Severn

When Blackhawk operative Vincent Kalani boarded an airplane, he never expected it to crash into the Alaskan mountains, but by-the-book police officer Shea Ramsey soon becomes his unlikely partner in survival. Can they escape the wilderness, or will their attackers find them first?

#1956 MARINE PROTECTOR
Fortress Defense • by Julie Anne Lindsey

Pursued by a madman, single mom Lyndy Wells and her infant son are bodyguard Cade Lance's priority assignment. Cade knows they must find the serial killer quickly or Lyndy and her baby will face grave danger. And Cade won't let that happen on his watch.

#1957 WITNESS SECURITY BREACH
A Hard Core Justice Thriller • by Juno Rushdan

There's not a target out there that US Marshals Aiden Yazzie and Charlotte "Charlie" Killinger can't bring down. Until a high-profile witness goes missing and a fellow marshal is murdered. Can they steer clear of temptation to find their witness before it's too late?

#1958 STALKED IN THE NIGHT
by Carla Cassidy

The target of a brutal criminal, Eva Martin is determined to defend her son and her ranch. Jake Albright is a complication she doesn't need—especially since he doesn't know about their child. As danger escalates and a shared desire grows, can Eva hold on to the family she's just regained?

SPECIAL EXCERPT FROM

⊕HARLEQUIN
INTRIGUE

When Blackhawk operative Vincent Kalani boarded an airplane, he never expected it to crash into the Alaskan mountains, but by-the-book police officer Shea Ramsey soon becomes his unlikely partner in survival. Can they escape the wilderness, or will their attackers find them first?

Read on for a sneak preview of
The Line of Duty *by Nichole Severn.*

He had a lead.

The partial fingerprint he'd lifted from the murder scene hadn't been a partial at all, but evidence of a severe burn on the owner's index finger that altered the print. He hadn't been able to get an ID with so few markers to compare before leaving New York City a year ago. But now, Blackhawk Security forensic expert Vincent Kalani finally had a chance to bring down a killer.

He hauled his duffel bag higher on his shoulder. He had to get back to New York, convince his former commanding officer to reopen the case. His muscles burned under the weight as he ducked beneath the small passenger plane's wing and climbed inside. Cold Alaskan air drove beneath his heavy coat, but catching sight of the second passenger already aboard chased back the chill.

"Shea Ramsey." Long, curly dark hair slid over her shoulder as jade-green eyes widened in surprise. His entire body nearly gave in to the increased sense of gravity pulling at him had it not been for the paralysis working through his muscles. Officer Shea Ramsey had assisted Blackhawk Security with investigations in the past at the insistence of Anchorage's chief of police, but her form-fitting pair of jeans, T-shirt and zip-up hoodie announced she wasn't here on business. Hell, she was a damn beautiful woman, an even better investigator and apparently headed to New York. Same as him. "Anchorage Police Department's finest, indeed."

"What the hell are you doing here?" Shea shuffled her small backpack at her feet, crossing her arms over her midsection. The tendons between her shoulders and neck corded with tension as she stared out her side of the plane. No mistaking the bitterness in her voice. "Is Blackhawk following me now?"

"Should we be?"

Don't miss
The Line of Duty *by Nichole Severn,*
available October 2020 wherever
Harlequin Intrigue books and ebooks are sold.

Harlequin.com

HIEXP0920

Get 4 FREE REWARDS!

We'll send you 2 FREE Books plus 2 FREE Mystery Gifts.

WHAT SHE DID
BARB HAN
LARGER PRINT

HOSTILE PURSUIT
JUNO RUSHDAN
LARGER PRINT

Harlequin Intrigue books are action-packed stories that will keep you on the edge of your seat. Solve the crime and deliver justice at all costs.

FREE Value Over **$20**